THE DIARY OF A YOUNG GIRL

THE DIARY OF A YOUNG GIRL

Anne Frank

Om KIDZ
An imprint of Om Books International

Om KIDZ | Om Books International

Reprinted in 2023

Corporate & Editorial Office
A-12, Sector 64, Noida 201 301
Uttar Pradesh, India
Phone: +91 120 477 4100
Email: editorial@ombooks.com
Website: www.ombooksinternational.com

Sales Office
107, Ansari Road, Darya Ganj,
New Delhi 110 002, India
Phone: +91 11 4000 9000
Email: sales@ombooks.com
Website: www.ombooks.com

Retold by Swayam Ganguly

ISBN: 978-93-5376-675-7

Printed in China

10 9 8 7 6 5 4 3 2

Contents

Chapter One

The Unique Gift

JUNE 14, 1942

I hope I shall be able to confide everything to you, as I've never been able to confide in anyone. I also hope you shall provide me with great comfort and support. So far you have been a great source of comfort to me, and so has Kitty, whom I write to on a regular basis now. But this way of keeping a diary is so much nicer, and I can barely wait for those moments when I'm able to pen down my thoughts on you.

I shall start from the moment you came into my life, when I saw you lying on the table

Happy Birthday
Anne

with my other birthday presents. It was Friday, June 12, and I woke up at six a.m., which was not surprising as it was my birthday. But as I am not permitted to wake up so early, I had to hold my curiosity until quarter to seven. I went to the dining room first, where Moortje (the cat) gave me a warm welcome by rubbing her body against my legs.

After seven, I entered the living room to see my presents. You were the first thing that I saw, one of my nicest presents. After that I saw a bouquet of roses, a few peonies and a potted plant. Daddy and Mama gave me a blue blouse, a game, a bottle of grape juice that tasted a little like wine (wine is made from grape juice after all), a jar of cold cream, a puzzle, 2.50 guilders and a gift certificate for two books. I also got other presents like lots of candy and a strawberry tart from Mother. Granny sent me a letter, that arrived right on time. But that was just a coincidence.

Hanneli came to pick me up after that, and we left for school. During recess I handed over the homemade cookies that I had baked myself to my teachers and fellow students. As I went to gym with the rest of the class (I'm not permitted to take part as my hips and shoulders tend to get dislocated), I reached home only at five.

I got to choose which game my classmates would play as it was my birthday. I chose volleyball, and later, they danced around me in a circle, singing 'Happy Birthday.' Sanne Ledermann was already there when I reached home. Ilse Wagner, Hanneli Goslar and Jacqueline van Maarsen who are in the same class as me, came home with me after gym. Hanneli and Sanne were my two best friends, and people seeing us together used to say, "There go Anne, Hanne and Sanne."

I met Jacqueline van Maarsen only when I started at the Jewish Lyceum, and she's my best friend now. Ilse is Hanneli's best friend, and Sanne goes to another school and has friends there. They gifted me a beautiful book called *Dutch Sasas and Lesends* but gave me Volume II by mistake. So, I exchanged two other books I had for Volume I. Aunt Helene gave me a puzzle, Aunt Stephanie a darling brooch, and Aunt Leny a lovely book: *Daisy Goes to the Mountains.*

This morning, as I lay in the bathtub, I thought, *How wonderful it would be to have a dog like Rin Tin Tin. I'd take him to school with me, where he could stay in the janitor's room or by the bicycle racks if the weather was good.* My birthday party was on Sunday afternoon, and the Rin Tin Tin movie was a big hit with my classmates. I got two brooches, two books and a bookmark.

JUNE 20, 1942

I find writing in a diary a strange experience. This is not only because this is the first time I'm writing, but also because I feel that no one will be interested in the thoughts of a thirteen-year-old schoolgirl. Oh, well, it really doesn't matter! I feel like writing, and the need to get things off my chest is also greater.

'Paper has more patience than people'. I was reminded of this saying on a particularly depressing day. I was sitting at home, chin in my hands, bored and listless, wondering if I should step outdoors or stay indoors. Finally, I stayed where I was, pondering. Yes, paper does have more patience, and since I am not planning to have anyone else read my diary, unless I find a real friend, it won't make much of a difference.

The main reason for me to keep a diary is that I don't have a friend. But no one will believe that a thirteen-year-old girl is all alone in this world. I'm not! I have loving parents and a sixteen-year-old elder sister as family. I have thirty people I can call friends, and a throng of admirers who can't keep their eyes off me in a classroom. I have loving aunts and a good

home. I have everything except that one true friend. I just think about having a good time when I'm with friends and can only talk about normal everyday things. We don't get any closer, and that is the problem. Perhaps it's my fault that we don't confide in each other. But that's how things are, and unfortunately, they won't change.

I don't want to pen down the facts in this diary as most people do. I want the diary to be my friend that I never had, and I'm going to call this friend, Kitty. Much as I hate doing, I must provide a brief sketch of my life instead of diving right in and making it difficult for people to understand what I have written to Kitty.

My adorable and loving father married my mother when he was thirty-six and she was twenty-five. My sister Margot was born in Frankfurt, Germany, in 1926. I was born on June 12, 1929 and lived in Frankfurt till age four. As we are Jewish, my father immigrated to Holland in 1933 as the Managing Director

of the Dutch Opekta Company, a company manufacturing products to make jam. My mother, Edith Hollander Frank, accompanied him to Holland in September, and Margot and I were sent to stay with our grandmother in Aachen. Margot left for Holland in December, and I went in February as a birthday present for Margot.

I joined the Montessori nursery school immediately, and stayed there till I was six, when I started first grade. Mrs. Kuperus, the principal, was my teacher in the sixth grade. We were both in tears as we bid goodbye to each other at the end of the year. I had been accepted at the Jewish Lyceum, where Margot was already studying.

Our lives were not rosy, as our relatives in Germany were a victim of Hitler's anti-Jewish laws. Post the 1938 pogroms, my maternal uncles escaped from Germany to seek refuge in North America. My seventy-three-year-old grandmother arrived to live with us.

NEDERLANDS
EETGELEGENHEID
NETHERLANDS RESTAURANT
JODEN NIET TOEGESTAAN
JEWS ARE NOT ALLOWED

May 1940 brought bad times; there was the war to begin with, followed by the capitulationand the arrival of the Germans. That's when the trouble began for the Jews. A series of anti-Jewish decrees severely curbed our freedom: Jews were required to wear a yellow star and turn in their bicycles. They were banned from using streetcars or even ride in any car, including their own. They had to do their shopping between 3 and 5 p.m. and could only visit Jewish-owned barbershops and beauty parlours. Jews were forbidden to be out on the streets between 8 p.m. and 6 a.m., and could not attend theatres, movies or any form of entertainment. They could not use tennis courts, swimming pools, hockey fields or any other athletic field. Jews could not sit in their gardens after 8 p.m., could not visit Christian homes, and could only attend Jewish schools.

Grandma fell sick in the summer of 1941 and had to have an operation. Hence, my birthday

passed with little celebration. In the summer of 1940, it was the same story on my birthday because the war had just ended in Holland. In January 1942, Grandma died. No one is aware how much I love her and miss her. My birthday was celebrated in 1942 to make up for the past, and Grandma's candle was lit, along with the rest.

The four of us are still doing well, and that brings us to the present date of June 20, 1942.

Yours, Anne

Chapter Two

Going into Hiding

JULY 5, 1942

Dearest Kitty,

Our entire class is shaking in its shoes. The reason is the upcoming meeting where the teachers will decide who gets promoted to the next grade and who will not. I'm only unsure about one subject, and that is math. Anyway, there's nothing to do but wait, and tell each other not to lose heart.

On Friday, the graduation ceremony in the Jewish Theater went as expected. My report card wasn't bad as I got one D, a C- in algebra

and B's in everything else, except for two B+s and two B-s. My parents are happy, but they are unlike other parents when it comes to grades. They never worry about report cards, whether they are good or bad. It doesn't matter to them till I'm healthy, happy, and don't talk back too much.

I'm exactly the opposite as I do not wish to be a poor student. The Jewish Lyceum accepted me on a conditional basis, and I was supposed to stay in the seventh grade at the Montessori School, but Jewish children were supposed to go to Jewish schools. Mr. Elte gave his consent finally, after a great deal of persuasion, to accept Lies Goslar and me.

My sister Margot has also received her report card. Her performance is brilliant, as usual. She's so smart that if we had such a thing as 'cum laude', she would have passed with honours. Father has been at home a lot recently as there's nothing for him to do in office. It must feel bad if you are not needed. Opekta has been

taken over by Mr. Kleiman. A few days ago, Father spoke about going into hiding, and told us it would be very tough for us to live isolated from the rest of the world. I asked him why he was speaking of this now.

"Well, Anne, we don't want the Germans to seize our belongings and neither do we want to fall in their clutches. So, we will leave quietly instead of being hauled away," he explained.

"When, Father?" I enquired. I was frightened because he sounded so serious. "Don't worry, Anne! We'll take care of everything. Just enjoy your life while you can!" he said reassuringly. That was it. Oh, may his words not come true for as long as possible.

Yours, Anne

JULY 8, 1942

Dear Kitty,

It seems ages since Sunday morning as so much has happened! It seems that the whole world

has turned upside down. But I'm still alive, as you can see, and that's the main thing. Let me tell you what happened on Sunday afternoon. The doorbell rang at three o' clock. I didn't hear it as I was out in the balcony reading. An agitated Margot appeared in the kitchen doorway a little later.

"Father has received a call-up notice from the SS," she whispered. "Mother has gone to see Mr. van Daan." (Mr. van Daan is Father's business partner and good friend.)

I was shocked! Everyone knows what a call-up means. Visions of concentration camps and solitary cells ran through my head. How could we let Father walk into such a fate?

"Of course, he's not going," Margot announced. "Mother's gone to Mr. van Daan to ask if we can shift to our hiding place tomorrow as the van Daans will accompany us. In total, there will be seven of us."

We didn't speak after that as the strangeness of the situation reduced us to silence. Then, the doorbell rang again. "Don't open the door!" Margot exclaimed. But then, we heard Mother and Mr. van Daan downstairs. They entered and shut the door behind them. Each time the doorbell rang, Margot and I had to tiptoe downstairs to check if it was Father. We didn't let anyone else in and soon, we were packed off to another room as Mr. van Daan wished to speak to Mother alone.

Margot revealed that the call-up was for her and not Father. I started crying at this second shock. Margot is sixteen, and it seems that they want to send away girls her age on their own. But thank God that she won't be going, as Father had mentioned that all of us would go into hiding. But where would we hide? In the city or the country? Indoors or outdoors? When, where and how? These questions hounded me!

Margot and I started packing all our important belongings into one schoolbag, and the first thing I put in was this diary. Father finally arrived home at five o' clock, and we called Mr. Kleiman to ask him to drop by that evening. Mr. van Daan got Miep, who promised to return that night, leaving with a bag full of clothes. It was very quiet in our apartment after that, and none of us felt like eating. It was hot, and everything felt rather strange.

Mr. Goldschmidt, a divorced man in his thirties, was our tenant in the big, upstairs room. Miep and Jan Gies arrived at eleven. Miep has worked for Father's company since 1933 and has become a close friend, along with her husband Jan. Once again, more clothes were stuffed into Miep's bag and Jan's deep pockets. They left at eleven-thirty.

I was very tired, and even though I was aware that it would be the last night on my own bed, I fell asleep instantly, not waking up before Mother roused me at five-thirty the next morning. Thankfully, it wasn't as hot as Sunday as it rained throughout the day. All four of us had so many layers of clothing on that it seemed that we were going to spend the night

in a refrigerator. No Jew in our position would dare to leave the house with a suitcase full of clothes. Hence, I wore two undershirts, three pairs of underpants, a dress, a skirt over that, a jacket, a raincoat, two pairs of stockings, heavy shoes, a cap, a scarf, and much more.

Stuffing her schoolbag with schoolbooks, Margot fetched her bicycle, and rode off into the great unknown, with Miep leading the way. I say this because I still didn't know where our hiding place was. We left at seven-thirty and I said bye to the only living creature left behind, Moortje, my cat. We left a note for Mr. Goldschmidt, to take her to the neighbours, so she would receive a good home.

Father, Mother and I walked in the pouring rain together, each carrying a schoolbag and a shopping bag full to the brim. People going to work at that early hour gave us looks of sympathy, and their faces reflected that they were sorry they couldn't provide us with some transportation. The conspicuous yellow star on

KANTOOR/OFFICIE
OFFICE

our clothes spoke for itself. Father and Mother slowly revealed their plan. For months, we had been moving our furniture and clothes out of our apartment slowly whenever we could. We had initially planned to go into hiding on July 16, but we preponed our plan to ten days earlier because of Margot's call-up notice. The hiding place was in Father's office building, and there were not too many people working there. There was Mr. Kugler, Mr. Kleiman, Miep and a twenty-three-year-old typist named Bep Voskuijl, who were all aware of our arrival.

Let me describe the building. The large warehouse on the ground floor serves as a workroom and storeroom and is divided into many different sections. Another outside door is next to the warehouse doors, a separate entrance to the office. A second door is just inside the office door, and a stairway lies beyond that. Another door is at the top of the stairs, with a frosted window on which 'Office' is written. This is the big front office which is huge, light and full. Bep, Miep and Mr. Kleiman work here during the day. The small, dark, stuffy back office was shared by Mr. Kugler and Mr. van Daan earlier, but now is used only by Mr. Kugler. One can also reach Mr. Kugler's office from the hallway, but only through a glass door that is easily opened from the inside, but not from the outside. Leaving Mr. Kugler's office and walking down the long, narrow hallway past the coal bin and going up four steps, you are in the private office, the showpiece of the entire building. It has a radio, a fancy lamp, elegant mahogany furniture, and throw rugs cover a linoleum floor. Everything is first class and a spacious kitchen with two gas burners and a hot-water heater lies just next door. A bathroom is beside that, and that's the second floor. A wooden staircase goes up to the third floor from the downstairs hallway. There is a landing with doors on either side at the top of the stairs. The left door leads to the spice storage area, attic and loft in the frontal area of the house. A characteristic Dutch, steep, ankle-twisting flight of stairs ascends from the frontal area of the house to another door that opens onto the street.

The door to the right of the landing takes you to the 'Secret Annex' at the back of the house. Who could suspect that there were so many rooms behind that plain, grey door? Just a small step in front of the door, and you're inside! A steep flight of stairs is before you, and to the left is a narrow hallway that leads to the Frank family's living room and bedroom. A smaller room lies next door serving as the bedroom and study of the two young ladies of the family. A windowless washroom with a sink is to the right of the stairs. The door in the corner leads to the toilet and another to Margot's and my room. Going up the stairs and opening the door at the top, one is greeted with the sight of a large, spacious and light room with a stove and a sink (because it used to be Mr. Kugler's laboratory). This is the kitchen and bedroom of

Mr. and Mrs. van Daan, and the living room, dining room and study for all of us. A small side room is Peter van Daan's bedroom. There's an attic and a loft as well.

After our arrival at 263 Prinsengracht, Miep led us into the Annex quickly, shut the door, leaving us alone. Margot was waiting for us, having arrived much earlier on her bike. All the rooms were packed with stuff. Cardboard boxes were piled on the beds and floor, and the small room was packed from floor to ceiling with linens. We had to clean up the mess if we had to sleep properly on beds that night. Mother and Margot lay on their bare mattresses, exhausted and miserable. But Father and I got to work right away. We unpacked boxes all day, filed cupboards, and cleaned up the mess till we fell in our beds, exhausted. We hadn't had a hot meal all day but didn't care as we were too busy to eat, just like Mother and Margot were too tired to. On Tuesday morning, we started where we had left off the night before. Bep and

Miep went grocery shopping armed with ration coupons, and Father and I cleaned up the mess till sundown. Till Wednesday, I didn't have a chance to reflect upon the huge change in my life. Then, for the first time since our arrival in the Secret Annex, I found the time to tell you all about it. It also dawned upon me what had happened and what was yet to take place.

Yours, Anne

Chapter Three

The van Daans

JULY 11, 1942

Dear Kitty,
I don't think I'll ever be at home in this house, although that doesn't mean I hate it. It's more of being on holiday in a strange mansion. It's an odd way to look at it, but it's exactly how it is. The Annex is a perfect place to hide in, despite being damp and lopsided. But there's probably no comfortable hiding place in all of Amsterdam.

Until now, our bedroom was rather bare thanks to its blank walls. Father had brought

my entire postcard and movie-star collection here before we arrived, and so, with the help of a brush and a pot of glue, I could plaster the wall with pictures. It looks much brighter now.

Margot and Mother have recovered a bit, and Mother was strong enough to cook split-pea soup for the first time. But then, she got busy talking downstairs, forgetting all about it. The beans were burnt black, and no amount of scraping could make them leave the pan.

Last night, the four of us went to the private office to listen to England on the radio. I was so frightened that someone else might hear it that I pleaded with Father to take me back upstairs. Mother understood my concern and accompanied me. We are very scared that the neighbours might hear or see us. The first day, we sewed curtains. I wonder why they call them that, as they're nothing but scraps of fabric, differing greatly in shape, pattern and quality. Father and I stitched in a haphazard way with our unskilled fingers. Our works of art were tacked to the windows, and they will remain there till we come out of hiding.

The building on our right is a branch of the Keg Company, a firm from Zaandam, and a furniture workshop is located on the left. Although the workers here are not present on the premises after work, any sound we make could travel through the walls. We've forbidden Margot from coughing at night, despite her bad cold, and are giving her large doses of codeine.

I'm looking forward to the van Daans' arrival here on Tuesday. It will be more fun and less quiet then. The silence here makes me nervous at night, and I'd love to have one of our helpers sleep here. But it's not so bad, as we can do our own cooking and listen to the radio. Mr. Kleiman, Miep and Bep Voskuijl have helped us a lot. We have canned lots of cherries, strawberries and rhubarb, and have a good supply of reading material. We also plan to buy lots of games. So, I doubt we'll be bored for the time being. Yes, we can't go outside or look out of the window and must be quiet, so people downstairs can't hear us. We had to pit two crates of cherries for Mr. Krugler to can yesterday. We plan to use the empty crates to make bookshelves.

Someone's calling me.

Yours, Anne

Comment added by Anne Frank on September 29, 1942: It is most upsetting that I'm unable to go outside, and I'm terrified that our hiding place will be discovered, and we'll be shot.

AUGUST 14, 1942

Dear Kitty,

I've deserted you for an entire month, but very less has happened to report every day. On July 13, the van Daans arrived, a day earlier because the Germans were sending out call-up notices left and right, causing a lot of fear.

We were still having breakfast when Peter van Daan arrived at nine-thirty. Peter's a shy,

awkward boy, who's sixteen years old. He won't be much of company. Mr. and Mrs. van Daan arrived half an hour later. We had our meals together from the beginning itself, and just after three days, it seemed that the seven of us had become one large family. Naturally, the van Daans had a lot to tell us about the week we had been isolated from civilisation. We were particularly interested to learn the outcome of our apartment and about Mr. Goldschmidt.

We laughed hard when Mr. van Daan related the incidents of people with vivid imaginations. For example, a family residing in our square claimed they saw all four of us riding on our bikes early in the morning. Another woman was sure that we had been boarded into a military vehicle in the middle of the night. Many houses are being searched for hidden bicycles, and Mr. Kugler suggested that it would be safer to have a bookcase built in front of the entrance to our hiding place. This swings out on its hinges and opens like a door

Mr. Voskuijl did the required carpentry work. It's a beautiful day outside. It's nice, hot and pleasant. Despite everything, we are enjoying the weather by lounging on the folding bed in the attic.

Yours, Anne

Chapter Four

Germans and Jews

SEPTEMBER 29, 1942

Dear Kitty,

You experience the strangest things when you're in hiding. We wash ourselves in a washtub simply because we do not have a bathtub. Hot water is available only in the lower floor office, and the seven of us take turns to utilise this great opportunity. But as all of us are modest, private people, each of has a preferred place to wash ourselves. Peter, for example, bathes in the office kitchen, despite it having a glass door. He tells us

not to walk past the kitchen for half an hour whenever he bathes.

Mr. van D. takes his bath upstairs, preferring the privacy of his own room, despite the discomfort of having to carry the hot water upstairs. Mrs. van D. has yet to take a bath, as she is still contemplating the best place for her to take one. Father prefers the private office, and Mother uses the kitchen behind a fire screen. Margot and I have chosen the front office to be our bathroom, scrubbing ourselves in the dark as the curtains are drawn on Saturday afternoon.

Then, Peter suggested that I use the spacious office bathroom as an alternative. Now, I can sit down, switch on the light, lock the door, and have a bath comfortably, without fear, without anyone's help, and without being noticed.

The plumber was working downstairs on Wednesday, shifting the water pipes and drains from the office bathroom to the hallway so that the pipes don't freeze in the cold winter. The plumber's visit was unfortunate as not only was the bathroom off-limits, but we were also not allowed to run any water throughout the day. Father and I solved the problem by creating a chamber-pot, using a canning jar. Canning jars were used during the day when the plumber was present, to answer our calls of nature. You can imagine how difficult it was for Miss Quack, Quack, Quack!

Yesterday, I had a terrible fright as the doorbell rang suddenly. I panicked as I thought that someone was coming to get us, if you know what I mean. But I was calmed down with the assurance that it was either pranksters or the mailman.

Peter can be amusing at times, and the one thing we have in common is that both of us like to dress up, making everyone laugh. One evening, Peter dressed in one of his mother's skin-tight dresses and me in his suit. I wore a cap, and he had a hat on. When we made our appearance, the grown-ups almost fell of laughing, and we had great fun too.

Yours, Anne

OCTOBER 9, 1942

Dear Kitty,

I have nothing but sad and depressing news today. Many of our Jewish friends and acquaintances are being carried away in droves. The Gestapo is treating them very badly and transporting them in cattle vans to Westerbork, the big camp in Drenthe, where all the Jews are being sent. It must be terrible there as the people hardly get anything to eat and drink. Miep told us about someone who had managed to escape from Westerbork. Water is available for only one hour per day, and only a single toilet and sink are available for thousands of people. Men and women sleep in the same room, and children and women mostly have their heads shaved. Escape is almost next to

impossible, and Jewish people are branded by their shaved heads.

If Holland is so bad, what about the uncivilised, faraway places where the Germansare sending the Jews? It can be assumed that most of them are being murdered. The English radio reports that Jews are being gassed. Maybe that's the quickest way to die!

I feel horrible. Miep's accounts of these horrors are heart wrenching, and Miep is also very depressed. The other day, for example, the Gestapo left an elderly, crippled Jewish woman on Miep's doorstep, while they left to find a car. The old woman was paralysed in fear because of the glaring searchlights, and the guns firing at the British planes flying overhead. But no one, including Miep, dared to let her in. The Germans are very generous when it comes to punishing people.

Bep is also very low as her boyfriend is being despatched to Germany. Each time the

planes fly overhead, she is scared that they will drop all the bombs on Bertus's head. He's not the only one who's being made to work in Germany forcefully. Trainloads of young men are being sent daily. Only a few manage to escape, by sneaking off when the trains stop at small stations. The term 'hostages' is the latest punishment reserved for saboteurs. Prominent and innocent citizens are imprisoned, awaiting their execution. If the Gestapo can't locate the saboteur, they just grab five hostages randomly, and line them up against the wall. They are termed as 'fatal accidents' as you read about their death in the newspapers. These Germans are fine specimens of humanity! Also, there are no bigger enemies than Germans and Jews on earth.

Yours, Anne

Chapter Five

The Eighth Person

OCTOBER 14, 1942

Dear Kitty,

Mother, Margot and I are best friends once again, and this is much better. Last night, Margot and I were lying in bed, side by side. It was terribly cramped, but that's what made it fun. Margot asked me if she could read my diary occasionally. "Parts of it," I replied, and asked about hers. She allowed me to read her diary as well. We spoke about the future, but when I asked her what she wanted to be when she grew up, she wouldn't speak. In fact, she

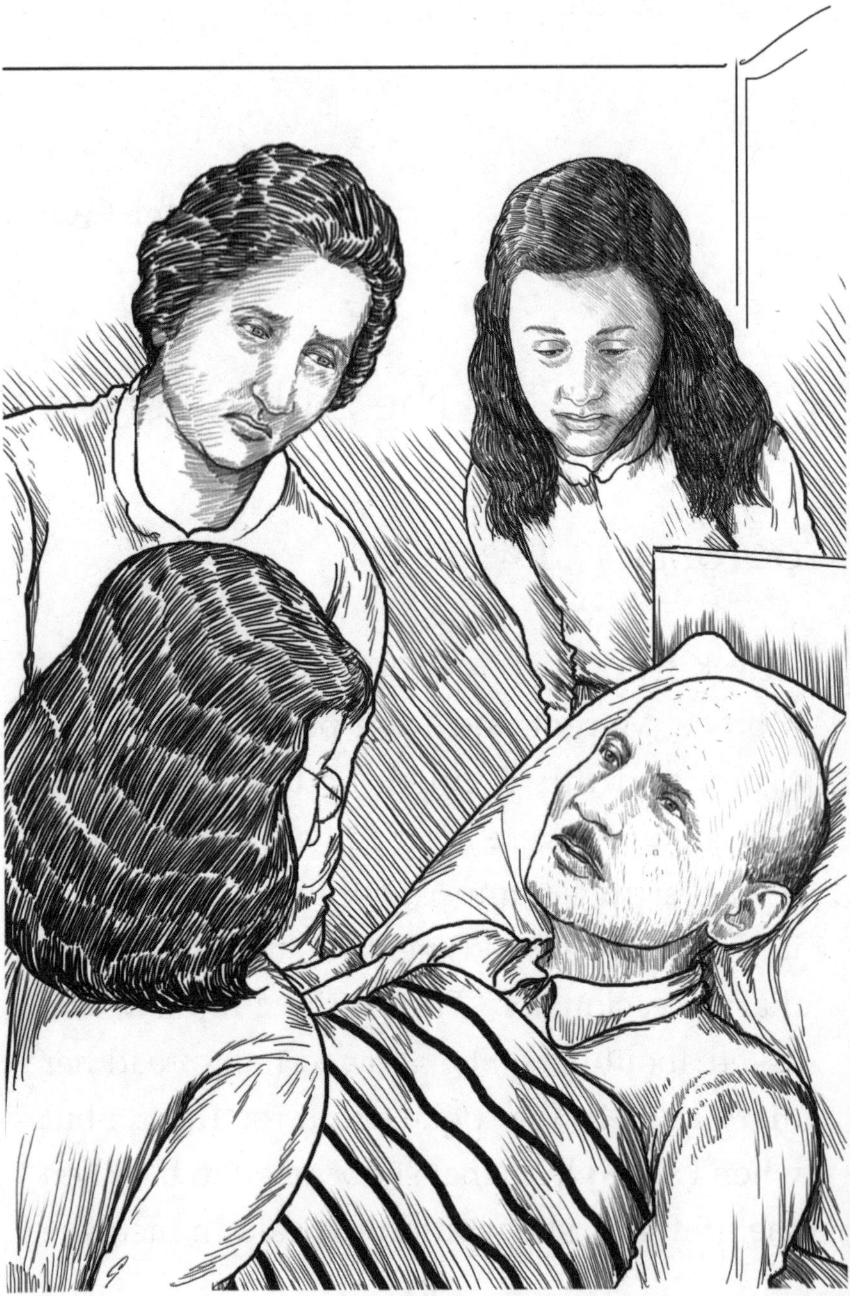

was rather mysterious about it. I guessed it had something to do with teaching, but I can't be sure. But I shouldn't be so nosy. Once, I asked Margot if she thought I was ugly. She replied saying I was cute and had nice eyes. That was a little vague, don't you think?

I'm really worried as Father's sick. He is running a high temperature and is covered with spots. It looks like measles, and just imagine, we can't even call a doctor! Mother is trying to make him sweat so that the fever goes out.

Father insists on me reading famous German writers like Hebbel and others. He's brought down the plays of Goethe and Schiller from the big bookcase, and intends to read to me every evening. We've begun with Don Carlos, and encouraged by Father, Mother has passed on her prayer book to me. To be polite, I read a few prayers in German. Although they do sound beautiful, they don't mean much to me. Why is she intent to make me so religious?

Tomorrow, we shall light the stove for the first time. The chimney hasn't been swept in years, so I'm sure that the room will be full of smoke. Here's hoping the thing draws!

Yours, Anne

NOVEMBER 9, 1942

Dear Kitty,

The British have finally met with success in Africa, although Stalingrad hasn't fallen yet. The men are happy, and we had coffee and tea this morning. Nothing else to report other than that.

Mother and I are getting along better but are never close. Although Father is not very expressive about his feelings, he is still the same dear old sweetheart. We lit the stove a couple of days ago and the room was full of smoke. Personally, I prefer central heating like many others. Margot's a stinker (no other word describes her better), a perpetual irritation, morning, noon and night.

Yesterday was Peter's sixteenth birthday, and he got a game of Monopoly, a razor and a cigarette lighter as presents. It's not that he smokes so much. In fact, it just looks so distinguished. Mr. van Daan surprised us all by declaring that the English had landed in Tunis, Algiers, Oran and Casablanca.

"This is the beginning of the end," everyone said. But here's what Churchill, the British Prime Minister, who must have heard the same thing being repeated, had to say, "This is not the end. It is not even the beginning of the end. But perhaps, it is the end of the beginning." Can you see the difference? But there is reason to be optimistic as Stalingrad, the Russian city under attack for three months, still hasn't fallen into German hands. Oh, I almost forgot to mention that Father has recovered from his illness.

The radio has just announced the fall of Algiers. England has taken control over Morocco, Oran and Casablanca for several

days. We are waiting for Tunis now. We are also awaiting the arrival of an eighth person to join our group in hiding. That's great news! We have always believed that there was room for one more person here but did not wish to burden Mr. Kugler and Mr. Kleiman further. But as reports of atrocities against the Jews were on the rise, Father decided to speak to the two gentlemen, and they thought it was an excellent plan. "It's equally dangerous, whether there are seven or eight," they observed rightly.

Then, we sat down to choose the one person who would join our group. After Father had rejected all the van Daan relatives, we froze on a dentist named Alfred Dussel. He is quiet and refined and appears to be nice. Miep knows him as well. If Mr. Dussel arrives, he will have to sleep in my room instead of Margot, who will have to use the folding bed. We must ask him to bring along something to fill cavities with, though.

Yours, Anne

NOVEMBER 17, 1942

Dear Kitty,

Miep arrived this morning to tell us that she had met Dr. Dussel. He asked Miep if she knew a hiding place and was thrilled when she said 'Yes.' Mr. Dussel's arrival was smooth. He was instructed by Miep to stand at 11 a.m. in front of the post office. Mr. Kleiman went to meet Mr. Dussel. Then, Mr. Kleiman took a streetcar back to the office, while Mr. Dussel followed on foot. Miep escorted Mr. Dussel upstairs. As she opened the bookcase and stepped inside, Mr. Dussel gaped in amazement. Meanwhile, the seven of us had seated ourselves around the dining table to welcome the new arrival with coffee and cognac. Mr. Dussel was so astonished that he sank into a chair when he was led upstairs. He looked at us in dumbstruck silence. "Aber...but you are nicht in Belgium? The officer, the auto, they were not coming? Your escape was not working?" he mumbled.

Everything was explained to him, including how we had spread the rumour about the officer and the car to throw the Germans off track. He was speechless! Then, we had lunch together. He took a short nap after that and joined us for tea. Eventually, he started feeling at home. Mr. Dussel is a nice man and didn't mind sharing a room with me at all. Honestly, I was not at all pleased by the thought of sharing my room with a stranger. But then, one must make sacrifices for a larger cause. On the first day, Mr. Dussel asked me all sorts of questions, like what time the cleaning lady arrived in the office, how we used the washroom, and the time when we are supposed to go to the toilet. He has spoken to us about the outside world. It is mostly sad news of our friends and acquaintances being taken away in green and grey military vehicles. These cruise the streets, knocking on every door, enquiring if any Jews live there. The entire family is taken away upon being discovered, and it's impossible to escape

them unless one goes into hiding. When it's dark, I often see long lines of innocent people marching slowly. Crying children accompany them, and the party is ordered about by a few men who beat and bully them till they almost drop. None are spared, including the sick, old, babies, and pregnant women as they are all marched to their death. We are lucky to be safe here. I get frightened to death when I think that my close friends are at the mercy of the cruellest monsters ever to walk this earth. And just because they're Jews.

Yours, Anne

Chapter Six

A Dental Appointment

NOVEMBER 28, 1942

Dear Kitty,

We have exceeded our ration of electricity, having used too much of it. The result is no light for fourteen days. But maybe it won't last so long! It gets too dark to read after four, and we must spend time doing silly activities like telling riddles, exercising in the dark, speaking French or English, and reviewing books. But everything gets boring after a while, and I discovered a new pastime yesterday. With the help of a good pair of binoculars, I peeked into the lighted rooms of the

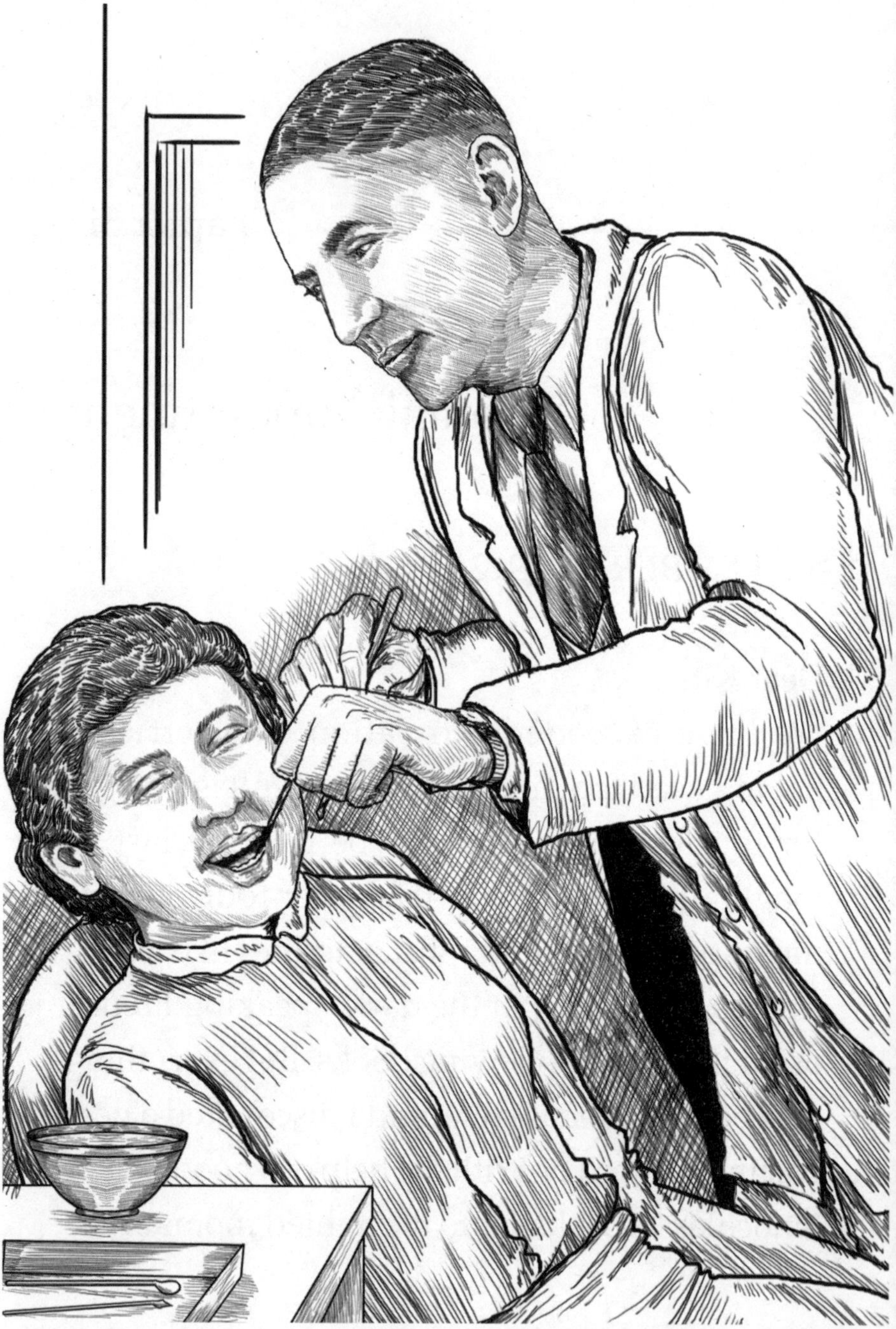

neighbours. Our curtains cannot be opened an inch during the day, but there's no harm in doing so at night. I'd never thought that our neighbours can be so interesting. I've discovered a family making home movies, and a dentist working on a scared old lady. Dussel has opened his own dental practice, and I shall describe his session with his first patient.

Mrs. van D was the first victim, seated on a chair in the middle of the room. Dussel assumed an air of importance as he unpacked his case. He asked for some eau de cologne, to be used as a disinfectant, and vaseline, as a substitute for wax. Exploring Mrs. van D's mouth, Dussel found two teeth that made her wince in pain and cry out each time he touched them. After a lengthy examination, (that's what Mrs. van D thought, as it took just two minutes), Dussel scraped out a cavity. Mrs. van D refused to let him do so and flailed her arms and legs till Dussel let go of his probe finally. But it remained stuck in her tooth, and she lashed out here and there wildly. Mrs. van D cried as much as one can with an instrument like that stuck in her mouth. She tried removing it, but only managed to push it in deeper.

Dussel observed the scene calmly, hands on his hips, while we roared with laughter. Of course, that was rather mean of us. I'm sure I'd have yelled even louder had I been in her place. Finally, after a lot of screaming, squirming, kicking and shouting, Mrs. van D managed to yank the offending instrument out, and Dussel carried on working as if nothing had happened. The patient was restless, and I bet it'll be a long time till she makes another dental appointment.

We have a new pastime, that is, filling packages with powdered gravy. Mr. Kugler still hasn't managed to find anyone to do this job, and it's also cheaper if we do it. This is the kind of job they do in prisons; it's terribly boring and makes us dizzy and giggly. Outside, terrible scenes can be witnessed as helpless people are dragged out of their homes and robbed off their possessions. Family members are separated from each other, and the Christians in Holland live in perpetual fear as their sons are being dispatched to Germany.

Each night, hundreds of planes fly over Holland, to drop their bombs on various German cities. Countless people are being killed in Russia and Africa, and no one can remain neutral in this conflict. The entire world is at war, and even though the Allies have a slight advantage, the end of this war is nowhere in sight.

In comparison, we are rather fortunate, and luckier than the others. It's safe and quiet here, and we are using our money to buy food. But we are selfish as we talk about buying new clothes and shoes after this war is over, when we should really be thinking about saving every penny to help the war victims. The children in this neighbourhood scamper about in thin shirts and wooden shoes. They do not have caps, stockings, coats. Neither do they have anyone to help them. They chew on carrots to satisfy their hunger

pangs and walk in the cold. Things in Holland have worsened so much that hordes of children stop people on the streets to beg for a piece of bread.

I could spend hours describing the misery this war has brought about, but that would only make me more miserable. All we can do is wait patiently and calmly for this nightmare to end. Jews and Christians are waiting together, and so is the entire world. Many are waiting for death!

Yours, Anne

JANUARY 30, 1943

Dear Kitty,

I'm burning with rage, yet I can't show it. I want to scream, shout, stamp my foot, shake Mother and cry, because of the nasty words she throws at me every day, piercing me like arrows. I want to scream at everyone here, and say, "Leave me alone. Give me one night where I don't have to cry myself to sleep. Let me get away from everything!"

We had a short circuit last night, and apart from that, the guns were booming away till dawn. I am still fearful about planes and shooting, and I still crawl into Father's bed almost every night. If that sounds childish, wait until it happens to you! The ack-ack guns make such a din that you can't even hear your own voice. It is worse in the dark than in candlelight. I was shivering, and begged Father to light the candle again. But he refused, as there was to be no light.

Then, there was the burst of machine-gun fire, which is ten times worse than anti- aircraft guns. Mother jumped out of bed, and much to Pim's (Father's pet name) annoyance, lit the candle.

"Anne is not an ex-soldier," was her reply to Father's constant grumbling.

Some German bigwig named Rauter gave a speech recently, "All Jews must evict German occupied territories before July 1. The province of Utrecht will be cleansed of Jews (as if we were cockroaches) between April 1 and May 1.

THE LABOUR EXCHANGE
DE ARBEIDSUITWISSELING

The same holds for North and South Holland provinces between May 1 and June 1."

Imagine these poor people being shipped off to dirty slaughterhouses like a herd of sick and neglected cattle. But I'll stop right here as my own thoughts give me nightmares.

There's some good news! In an act of sabotage, the Labour Exchange was set on fire. Then, the County Clerk's office went up in flames. Men disguised as German police bound and gagged the guards to destroy important documents.

Yours, Anne

Chapter Seven

Internal Conflicts

JUNE 15, 1943

Dear Kitty,

The doctor discovered that Mr. Voskuijl has cancer. It was in such an advanced stage that an operation was futile. So, they stitched him up again, and he was kept in the hospital for three hours. Then, they fed him and sent him back home. But they made the unforgivable error of disclosing to the poor man what was wrong with him.

He can't focus on work anymore, and just sits at home, thinking about his approaching

death, surrounded by his eight children. I am so sorry for him, and regret that I cannot go and meet him. Now, he cannot let us know what is happening in the warehouse which is sad for us. Mr. Voskuijl was our pillar of strength when it came to safety measures.

We must hand over our radio to the authorities next month. Mr. Kleiman has a small set hidden in his home, and he's giving us that to replace our lovely cabinet radio. It's sad that we must give away our big Philips, but when you're in hiding, you cannot afford to bring the authorities down on your trail. We'll put the 'baby radio' upstairs. The radio is a great source of encouragement as it tells us not to lose heart.

After a lot of thought, I've decided to drop the shorthand, so I can focus on my other subjects. It's also because of my eyes. I've become near-sighted and should have had glasses ages ago. (Ugh, I'll look like a dope) But people in hiding can't...

The British have landed in Sicily and Father's getting ready for a 'quick finish'. Bep has given me and Margot a lot of office work to do. Not only is it a big help to her but it also makes us feel important. Anyone can file letters and make entries in sales books, but we do it with incredible precision.

Miep has so much to carry that she resembles a pack mule. Almost every day, she leaves to gather vegetables, cycling back with large shopping bags. We long for Saturday as Miep gets five library books on Saturday, and we are like a bunch of little kids receiving gifts. Ordinary people are unaware how much books can mean to someone who's cooped up in a hole like us. The only diversions we have are reading, studying, and listening to the radio.

Sunday witnessed the heavy bombing of Northern Amsterdam with a lot of destruction. Entire streets lie in ruins, and it will take some time before all the bodies are dug out. Two hundred people have been reported dead and countless wounded. The hospitals are bursting at the seams. We've heard of crying children searching for their dead parents in the smouldering ruins, and that makes me shiver.

Let me tell you what each of us wants to do when we visit the outside world again. Margot and Mr. van Daan wish to have a hot bath over all else, lying in it for more than half an hour. Mrs. van Daan longs for a cake, and Dussel only wishes to see his Charlotte. Peter wishes to go downtown, Mother craves for a cup of real coffee and Father wants to visit Mr. Voskuijl. As for me, I'd be so happy that I wouldn't know where to begin. I'd love to have a home of our own above all else, so I can move around freely and where someone can help me with my homework. In other words, I'd love to return to school!

Bep has made an offer to fetch us some fruit at bargain prices: grapes 2.50 guilders a pound, gooseberries 70 cents a pound, one peach 50 cents, melons 75 cents a pound. No surprise

that the papers write every evening in big, fat letters: 'Keep Prices Down!'

Yours, Anne

JULY 26, 1943

Dear Kitty,

Yesterday was a hectic day, and we are still wound up. You might wonder if each day doesn't provide some sort of excitement. In the morning, the first warning siren went off while we were still at breakfast. But we paid no heed, as this signified that the planes were crossing the coast. I lay down for an hour after breakfast because of a splitting headache and left for the office around two.

Margot had finished her office work at two-thirty and was just collecting her things when the sirens sounded again. We rushed back upstairs together, and in just five minutes, the guns were booming so loudly that we sought refuge in the hall. As the bombs kept falling, the

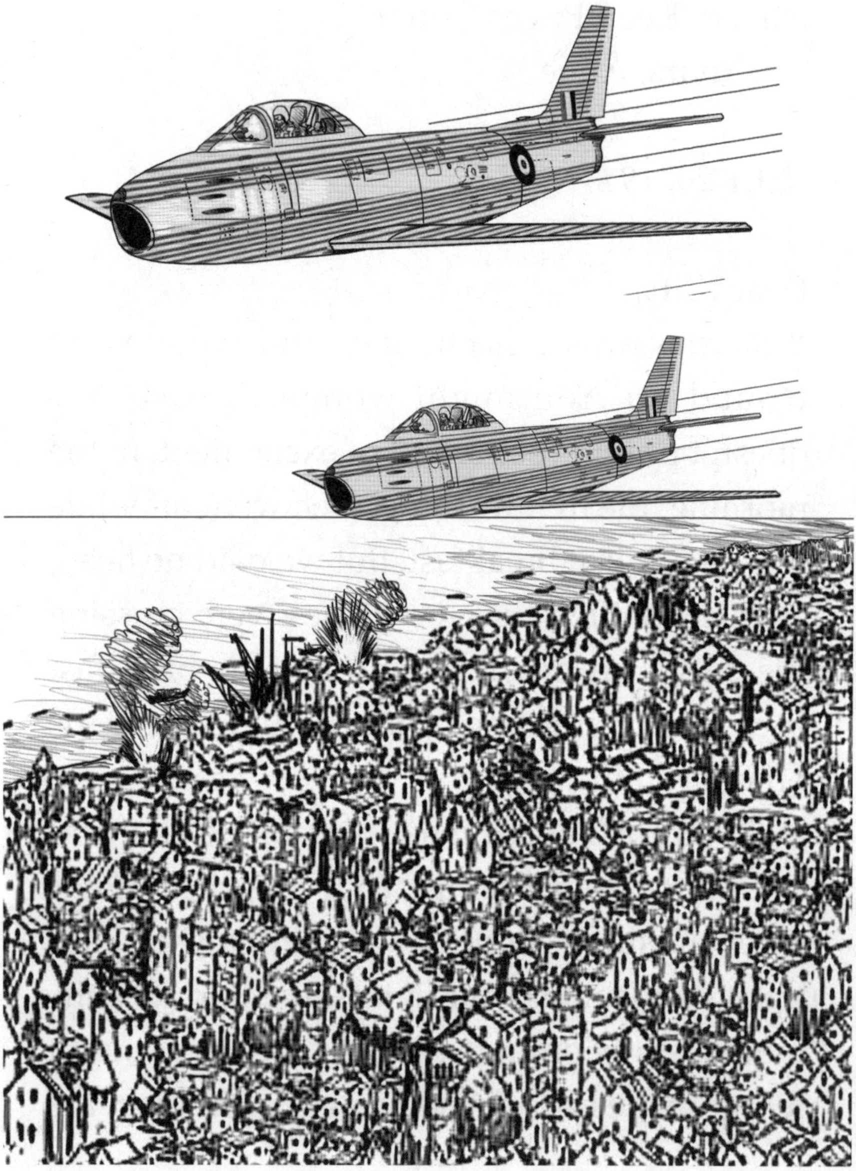

house shook. Thankfully, the drone of engines faded after half an hour, and the house throbbed with activity again.

Peter emerged from his lookout post in the attic while Dussel remained in the front office. Mrs. van D felt the private office to be the safest, and Mr. van D stayed in the loft. We watched columns of smoke rising from the harbour and soon the smell of fire was everywhere. The city appeared to be gripped by a thick fog.

It appeared to be over, but just as we began dinner, another air-raid alarm sounded. I lost my appetite the minute I heard it. But nothing happened, and the all clear was sounded after forty-five minutes. But just after the dishes had been washed, an air-raid warning was followed by gunfire and planes.

Oh God! Twice in one day! we thought.

Bombs rained down on the other parts of the city, and Schiphol Airport was bombed, according to British reports. I was very

frightened, and thought all the time, "Here it comes, this is it."

My legs were still shaking when I went to bed at nine, and the sound of more planes woke me up at midnight. I jumped up and stayed in Father's bed till one. Then, I was at my own bed till one-thirty, and back in Father's bed again at two. I finally fell asleep at two-thirty when the chaos stopped. I woke up with a start at seven to see Mr. van Daan with Father. It was wonderful news, the best since the war began. Mussolini has resigned, and the King of Italy has taken over the government.

Mr. Kugler visited us to inform that the Fokker aircraft factory had been hit hard. There was another air-alarm this morning, and these alarms have killed my sleep and peace. I've hardly slept, but now the suspense about Italy and the hope that the war will end soon are keeping us awake.

Yours, Anne

AUGUST 3, 1943

On the political front, things are going well as the Fascist Party has been banned by Italy. In many places, the people are at war against the Fascists, and the army has also joined the fight. How can a country like that afford to be at war with England?

Our lovely radio was confiscated last week and Dussel was very angry at Mr. Kugler for turning it in. Dussel has gone down in my estimation of him and is already below zero. His views on politics, history, geography and other things are too ridiculous to be repeated: Hitler will fade away from history; the harbour in Rotterdam is bigger than the Hamburg harbour; the English are idiots for not bombing Italy to destruction, etc., etc.

After the third air raid that just happened, I decided to grit my teeth and be braver. Mrs. van Daan, who always makes a pretence of being brave, is the most cowardly amongst us.

She was shaking in fear this morning and burst into tears. Her husband, with whom she is on good terms now after a week's quarrelling, comforted her.

But the bad news is about Mr. Kleiman. We all like him because of his cheerful and brave disposition. This is a constant even though he is sick, in pain, and can't eat or walk much. Mother says, "When Mr. Kleiman enters a room, the sun shines," and she's absolutely right. Now, it appears that he must go to the hospital for a difficult operation on his stomach and stay there for four weeks. He was normal when he said goodbye to us as if he were going on an errand.

Relationships here at the Annex are worsening, and we are quiet during meals as no matter what is said, it might rub someone the wrong way. Mr. Voskuijl comes to visit us sometimes, and he's not doing well unfortunately. But his attitude of 'What do I care? I'm going to die anyway!' is not making

it easier for his family. I wonder if people are so touchy here, what would it be like in the Voskuijl family? Another scary thing is the fact that Mr. van Maaren, the man working in the warehouse, is getting increasingly suspicious about the Annex. He's known to be suspicious, highly curious and unreliable.

Yours, Anne

Chapter Eight

Ghosts from the Past

OCTOBER 17, 1943

Dear Kitty,

Thank goodness, Mr. Kleiman is back! Even though he looks a bit pale, he smilingly left to sell clothes for Mr. van Daan. The problem is that Mr. van Daan has run out of money! He lost his last hundred guilders in the warehouse. The others are suspicious how a hundred guilders could land up in the warehouse on a Monday morning. But if they have been stolen, who's the thief? The money shortage cannot be solved as Mrs. van Daan refuses to part with her dresses,

coats and shoes. Mr. van Daan's suit is not easy to sell, and no one wants Peter's bike. Everyone in the house is on the edge, and I can only study to take my mind off it. Mr. Kleiman's stomach is giving him a lot of trouble, and he's also unaware if it has stopped bleeding. He left for home after telling us that he wasn't feeling well. I'm all right, except that I've lost my appetite. They are giving me calcium, dextrose, cod-liver oil, and brewer's yeast to keep me fine. I lose my nerves especially on Sundays and become miserable. The atmosphere outside is grim and oppressively silent. You can't even hear a bird! I feel like a songbird whose wings have been chopped off, and who flings itself against the bars of its dark cage, screaming, "Let me out to where there's fresh air and laughter"! I sleep on the divan as sleep makes the silence and the fear disappear quickly. It also helps pass the time as you just can't kill it.

Yours, Anne

NOVEMBER 17, 1943

Dear Kitty,
Recent events have shaken the very foundations of the house. Bep cannot meet us for six weeks because of an outbreak of diphtheria at her house. In her absence, the shopping and cooking will be difficult, and we'll miss her company too. Mr. Kleiman is still in bed, eating only gruel for three weeks, and Mr. Kugler is neck-deep in work.

Hanneli came to me last night just before I fell asleep. I saw her dressed in rags, her face pale and haggard. She stared at me with reproach and sadness in her eyes, in which the message was clear: "Oh Anne, why have you left me and gone? Help me! Rescue me from this hell"! But I can't help her. I can only watch as people suffer and die. I can only pray to God to return her. I saw no one else but Hanneli and I realised why. I misjudged her, being immature to judge how tough it was for her. She must

have felt that the girlfriend she was devoted to was trying to take her away. How awful the poor thing must have felt! It was mean of me having treated her that way, and now she was looking at me so helplessly. Oh, only if I could help her! Dear God, why have I been chosen to live if she was more faithful than me? Why are we separated?

Dear Hanneli, I hope you survive till the end of the war and return to us for me to undo the wrong I have done to you. I must stop thinking about her, but I keep seeing her huge eyes that haunt me. Oh Hanneli, if only I could help you! But it's too late now.

Yours, Anne

Chapter Nine

An Imperfect Mother

DECEMBER 24, 1943

Dear Kitty,

I couldn't write to you all this while because of a bad case of flu. Being sick here is the worst thing to happen, as I must duck under the blanket with every cough and try to prevent my coughing bouts from happening. I had to drink milk with honey, sugar or cough drops to make the tickle go away. I'm itching to get back to my books. Moods do affect us a lot here, and my moods are getting worse lately. I feel lucky when I compare myself to other Jewish children,

but I'm very sad when Mrs. Kleiman drops by and talks about Jopie's hockey club, canoe trips, school plays and afternoon teas. I don't think I'm jealous of Jopie, but I do wish I could have a good time too, and laugh till it hurts. We are like lepers in this house, especially during winters, Christmas and New Year. Whenever someone comes in from outside, I can't help from wallowing in despair, and thinking, *When will we breathe in the fresh air again?*

Trust me, if you have been confined indoors for a year and a half, it can get to you sometimes. But if all eight of us would make our discontent evident, would that really get us anywhere? I can cry and that can bring relief, but not when you cry alone! I miss having a mother who understands me. I imagine the kind of mother I'd like to be. The kind who doesn't take what people say too seriously, but who takes me seriously. The word 'Mom' says it all, and that's why I don't call my mother 'Mom'. I call her 'Momsy' often. I sometimes shorten it

to 'Moms', an imperfect 'Mom'. I wish I could honour her by removing the 's'. Thank God she doesn't realise this as it would make her sad. Enough of that! My writing has saved me from drowning in despair.

Yours, Anne

DECEMBER 29, 1943

Dear Kitty,

I was very sad last night as Grandma and Hanneli visited me again. Oh, my sweet Grandma! Little did we understand her deep suffering, her kindness, and her concern and interest towards us, all the while closely guarding her terrible secret! Grandma was too good and loyal to let us down. She would stick up for me no matter how badly behaved I was. Did you love me, Grandma, or did you not understand me either? How lonely you must have been despite our presence? Thinking about the suffering of your loved ones can reduce you to tears, and you can cry all day! All you can do is pray to God to perform a miracle and save at least some of them. I hope I'm doing enough of praying!

Yours, Anne

JANUARY 2, 1944

Dear Kitty,

I was free this morning and decided to go through the pages of my diary. I was shocked to discover many letters upon the subject, 'Mother' in such strong terms. *Anne is that really you talking about so much hate?* I said to myself. *Is that really you?*

I wondered how there was so much anger and hatred within me that I had to share it with all of you. I tried to understand the Anne of last year and apologise on her behalf because if I don't explain these accusations my conscience won't be clear.

Because of my moods then and now, I saw things only from my own perspective.

I never considered the others whom I had hurt or offended. I hid in my shell, and wrote everything down in my diary which means a lot to me as it is my memory book.

I was very angry at Mother (I still am mostly). We didn't understand each other, and she loved me to be kind towards me. But because of the sad circumstances we were in and the difficult situations I caused for her, she was often irritable and nervous. So, she was often angry with me. I took it to heart much more than I should have and retaliated in a nasty manner that made her unhappier. We were gripped by a vicious circle of sadness and displeasure. It was not a happy period for us, but thankfully it is coming to an end.

My violent outbursts on paper are just expressions of rage that I would have controlled in normal circumstances by locking myself in my room, stamping my foot a couple of times, or calling Mother a few names behind her back.

But the phase of passing judgments on Mother is over now. Mother has steadied her nerves a bit and I'm much wiser now. I manage to keep quiet when I'm annoyed, and so does she. So, at least we appear to be getting along well on the surface. But one thing I'm incapable of, is loving Mother with the devotion of a child. I thought it was better to pen down these unkind words for Mother in my diary rather than for her to carry around in her heart.

Yours, Anne

Chapter Ten

The Food Crisis

JANUARY 12, 1944

Dear Kitty,
It's been two weeks since Bep has returned. But her sister won't be allowed to attend school till next week. Bep spent two days in bed nursing a bad cold herself, and Miep and Jan were down for two days as well, with upset stomachs.

Currently, I'm experiencing a dance and ballet craze, and religiously practising my dance steps every evening. Using Momsy's lacy lavender slip, I've created an ultra modern dance costume. I've threaded bias tape through

A Cloudless Morning

the top and tied it just above the bust. The ensemble has been completed by a pink corded ribbon. I failed to transform my tennis shoes into ballet slippers, though. My stiff limbs are about to become as limber as they were. A great exercise is to sit on the floor, put a heel in each hand, and raise both legs in the air. I must sit on a cushion though, to protect my poor backside.

Everyone in the house is reading a book named 'A Cloudless Morning'. Mother thought it was particularly good as it addresses adolescent problems. *Why don't you take more interest in your own adolescents first?* I thought ironically. Maybe, Mother believes that Margot and I share a better relationship with our parents than anyone else in the world, and that she is the most dedicated mother. She must be thinking about Margot in her belief, as Margot does not have the problems with Mother, as I do. Even if I point out to Mother what I think, it wouldn't help. She would be stunned, and besides, I don't think she can ever change.

I'd like to avoid her being pained as I'm sure nothing will change. I think she is aware that Margot loves her more than I do. But she also thinks that I'm going through a phase.

Margot's much nicer now and a lot different from earlier. She's become a real friend and does not consider me as a little kid. Recently, I've developed a liking for family trees as well as the genealogical tables of royal families. I've concluded that as you dig deeper into your past, the discoveries become more and more interesting. Although I ensure that my studies are never neglected, I also follow the BBC Home Service on the radio. I spend most of my Sundays sorting and looking at my movie-star collection, which is impressive now. Mr. Kugler increases my happiness by bringing me a copy of the Cinema & Theatre magazine every Monday.

The less passionate family members term this as a waste of money but are surprised at the accuracy with which I can list the actors in any movie, year after year. Bep goes to the movies with her boyfriend every Saturday, on her day off. She tells me the name of the movie she's going to, and I rattle off the names of the actors and actresses as well as the reviews. Moms said that I wouldn't need to see these movies later, as I knew everything by heart already. I can spot the disapproval in their faces whenever I sport a new hairstyle. I'm sure they'll ask me which movie star I'm trying to copy. When I invent my own reply, that's met with scepticism. The hairdo doesn't last for more than half an hour though, as tired of their remarks, I rush to the bathroom and restore my hair to its original mass of curls.

Yours, Anne

MARCH 10, 1944

Dear Kitty,
The proverb 'Misfortunes never come singly' certainly holds good for today. Peter just

Butte

finished saying it. Let me put into writing all the dreadful things that have happened today and still loom over our heads. Firstly, Miep is unwell. She caught a cold in Westkerk, where Henk and Aagje's wedding service was held yesterday. Secondly, Mr. Kleiman hasn't joined back work since his stomach started bleeding. Hence, Bep has had to hold fort all alone. Then, the police have arrested a man (I won't put his name in writing) who has been supplying us with potatoes, jam and butter. Not only is it terrible for us, but also for him as he has five children, with another on the way. We had a scare last night when someone knocked on the wall next door as we were having dinner. We were tense and nervous for the rest of the evening.

Recently, I have not been in the mood to write down everything happening here because I'm too involved in myself. Don't get me wrong as I'm really upset about what happened to poor Mr. M. But there's little room for him in my

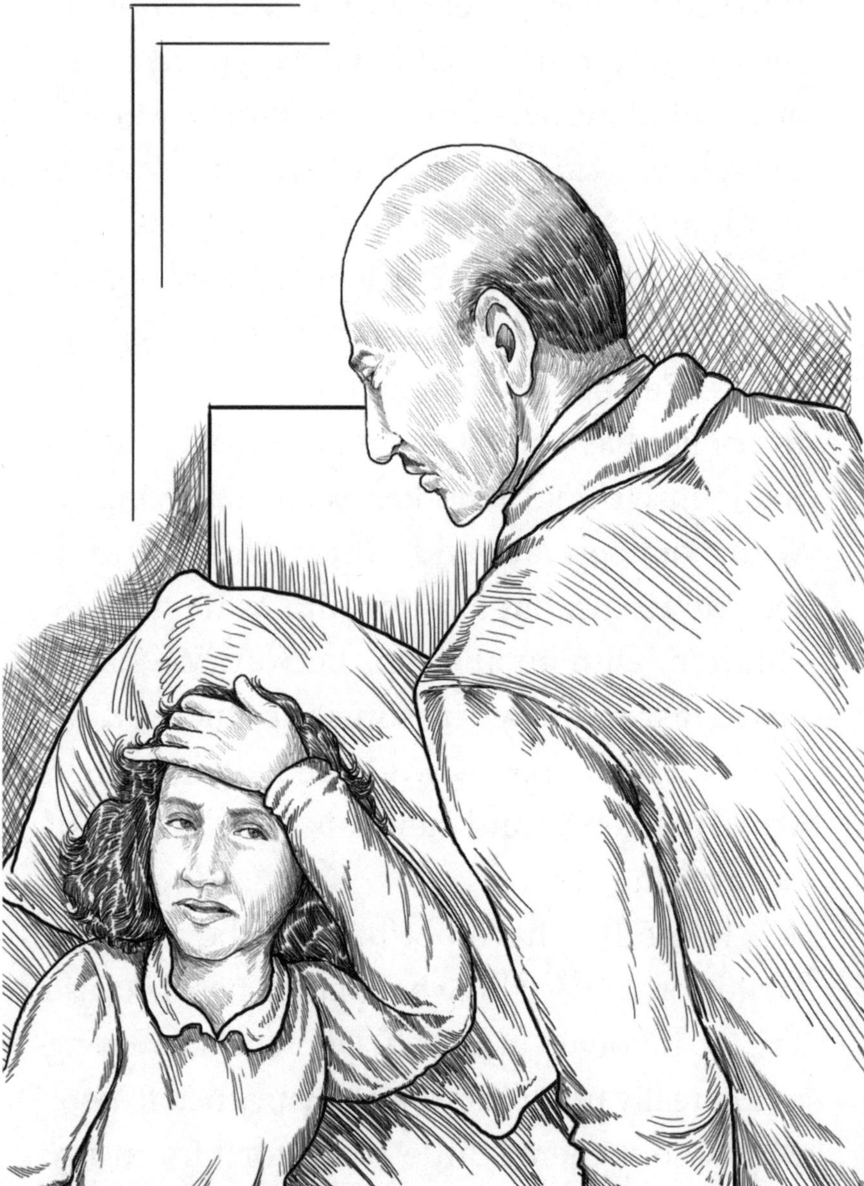

diary. Things are getting crazier here with each passing day. I have a tough time pretending everything is normal and acting cheerful when I'm feeling so sad. I miss the outdoors the most.

Yesterday afternoon, I was feeling so wretched that I lay down on the divan for a nap. I wanted to sleep so that I didn't have to think. I slept till four, but I had to go next door after that. It was difficult answering Mother's questions, and explaining my nap to Father. I told him I had a headache, which wasn't exactly a lie, as I had one on the inside!

Ordinary girls who are teenagers like myself might think that I'm crazy with all my self-pity. But that's the way it is. I pour my heart out to you, but the rest of the time I'm as cheerful and self-confident as I can be to avoid questions, and not get on my own nerves. Margot is very kind and hopes that I would confide in her. But I can't tell her everything. She takes me way too seriously and devotes a lot of time thinking about her loony sister.

Is she acting, or does she really mean it? Margot wonders. That's because we are always together. I don't want the person I confide in to be around me all the time. How will I untangle my mixed-up thoughts otherwise? How shall I find inner peace again?

Yours, Anne

MARCH 14, 1944

Dear Kitty,

You might find it amusing (I don't) what we are going to eat today. As the suppliers providing us with food coupons have been arrested, all we have is our five black-market ration books. We have no coupons, fats, and oils. Miep and Mr. Kleiman are sick again, and Bep can't manage the shopping. The food is awful and so are we. We won't have a bit of fat, margarine or butter tomorrow. It's not possible to have fried potatoes for breakfast anymore (we've been doing that to save bread) and so, we're having hot cereal instead. We bought some half-and-half as Mrs. van D thinks we're starving. Lunch comprises mashed potatoes and pickled kale today, and you can't imagine how much kale stinks when it's a few years old. The kitchen smells like a mixture of rotten eggs, brine and spoiled plums. Ugh! Just the thought of eating that muck makes me want to throw up! Honestly, being in hiding during the fourth year of the war is no joke. It's no picnic either, and I wish this stinking mess was over soon.

The food wouldn't have been so unpleasant if life was pleasant here. But this difficult existence has made us all unpleasant. As children aren't allowed to express their opinions, here are the opinions of the five grown-ups on the present scenario. For once, I'm following the rules.

Mrs. van Daan: "I'd have given up wanting to be queen of the kitchen a long time ago. But as sitting around and doing nothing was boring, I returned to cooking. Though I can't help but complain as it's impossible to cook without oil, and those repulsive smells make me sick. Also, what do I get in return for my efforts? Rude remarks and ungratefulness! I am the black sheep here who gets blamed for everything. I also think that this war is making little progress, and that the Germans will emerge victorious in the end. I'm scared we will starve to death, and I snap at everyone in my bad mood".

Mr. van Daan: "All I do is smoke. The political situation, Kerli's mood swings and the food don't feel so bad then. Kerli's a sweetheart. But I get sick if I cannot smoke, and then I feel the need to consume meat. Life becomes unbearable then, and nothing is good enough. There are rows. My Kerli's an idiot"!

Mrs. Frank: "Right now, food is not so important, but I'm so hungry, I'd love a slice of rye bread! I'd have stopped Mr. van Daan's smoking a long time ago had I been in Mrs. van Daan's place. But now, I long for a cigarette myself as my head's in a twirl. I think the van Daans are horrible. The war

is making progress although the English are making many mistakes. But I'm grateful I'm not in Poland".

Mr. Frank: "I'm absolutely fine and I don't need anything. We should stay calm as there's plenty of time. I'm silent as long as I have my potatoes. I'd better set aside some of my rations for Bep. I'm very optimistic as I think the political situation is improving".

Mr. Dussel: "I must complete the task I've set out to do as it's important that everything be finished on time. It's impossible for us to be captured and the political situation is looking 'gut'. Me, me, me..."

Yours, Anne

Chapter Eleven

Amsterdam Burning

MARCH 16, 1944

Dear Kitty,
What a relief it is to be released from the gloom and doom for a few moments! The only thing that I've been hearing all day is: "If this and that happens, we'll land up in trouble, and if so-and-so gets sick, we'll be left alone to take care of ourselves, and if…"

The reason for all the 'ifs' cropping up is that Mr. Kugler has been summoned for a six-day work detail, Bep is in bed with a bad cold and will probably stay indoors tomorrow, Miep hasn't

recovered from her flu, and Mr. Kleiman lost consciousness because of his bleeding stomach.

We all think that Mr. Kugler should visit a good doctor for a medical certificate of ill health which can be presented to the City Hall in Hilversum. The warehouse employees have been given the day off tomorrow, and Bep will be alone in office. Another 'if' is if Bep must stay at home, the door must remain locked, and we must be absolutely quiet so that the Keg Company wouldn't hear us. Jan will arrive at one o' clock for half an hour to check on us just like a zookeeper checks on animals.

This afternoon, Jan gave us some news of the outside world for the first time in many months. His grateful audience was entertained with stories of- what else? - food. Mrs. P, a friend of Miep's has been making his meals. Jan had carrots with green peas the day before yesterday, had the leftovers yesterday, and today she's cooking marrow fat peas. Tomorrow she intends to mash the remaining carrots with potatoes. We enquired after Miep's doctor.

"What doctor?" Jan stated. "I called him this morning and got his secretary on the line. When I asked for a flu prescription, I was instructed to pick it up between eight and nine tomorrow morning. In case of a particularly bad case of flu, the doctor comes to the phone himself and says, "Stick out your tongue and say 'Aah'. Ooh, I can hear your infected throat. I'll write out a prescription and you can fetch it to the pharmacy. Have a good day!" That's that! Easiest job, diagnosis by phone. But I can't blame the doctor as he has only two hands and as of today, the patients outnumber the doctors.

We had a good laugh at Jan's phone call. I can almost visualise what a doctor's waiting room looks like these days. Doctors don't turn up their noses at poorer patients anymore, but at those with minor illnesses. "What on earth are you doing here?" they say. "Go to the end of the line! Real patients have to be prioritised!"

Yours, Anne

MARCH 16, 1944

Dear Kitty,

The weather is beautiful, indescribably gorgeous. I'll be going up the attic soon. I realise now why I'm more restless than Peter. He has his own room where he can think, work, sleep, and dream while I'm being constantly pushed around from corner to corner. I can never find privacy in the room I share with Dussel, even though I crave for it. That's one of the reasons for seeking refuge in the attic. I can be myself when I'm there or with you, dear Kitty, even though it's momentary. Yet, I don't want to complain, and want to be brave instead.

It's good that others don't notice my restlessness, although I'm more and more contemptuous of Mother now, less loving towards Father, and less inclined to share any thought with Margot. I'm closed tighter than a drum. Above everything, I've to maintain my air of confidence. No one must gauge that my

heart and mind are perpetually at war with each other. Reason has won the war so far, but will my emotions gain the upper hand ever? I fear they will, but I also hope they do! The best part is being able to write down these feelings; otherwise they'd suffocate me.

Thankfully everything's turned out right as Bep's just had a sore throat and not the flu. Mr. Kugler has received a medical certificate to excuse himself from the work detail. The entire Annex is relieved. The only thing is that Margot and I are tired of our parents. Don't get me wrong as I still love Father and Margot loves both our parents equally. But when you are as old as we are, certain decisions must be made by us alone by getting out from under their thumb. They ask me what I'm going to do each time I want to go upstairs. They won't let me salt my food and every evening at eight-fifteen, Mother wants me to change into my nighty. They must approve each book I read, and both Margot and I are tired of their questions and preaching all day long.

Also, the fact that I'm not giving them little kisses every morning, noon and night, displeases them. But I don't feel like doing something so childish. Father's fascination about farting and talking about it is so repulsive. I long to be away from their company for a while, and they don't understand this. We are treated like children even though we are more mature than girls our age, who are not treated this way. Even though I'm fourteen, I know the difference between right and wrong, and I also know what I want to do. I have my own set of ideas, principles and opinions, and even if it sounds strange, am more adult than child. I can debate better than Mother, make conversation better, am more objective and not prone to exaggeration. I'm much tidier at work with the hands, and much superior to Mother in many ways. (Even if that makes you laugh.)

I need to admire and respect a person to love that person. Sadly, I feel neither admiration nor respect for Mother.

Yours, Anne

MARCH 23, 1944

Dear Kitty,

Things are almost normal here now. Thank God our coupon men have been released from prison! Miep returned yesterday, but unfortunately her husband has fever now, and the symptoms indicate flu. Bep is much better, even though her cough's still there. But I'm afraid Mr. Kleiman must stay at home for a long time.

A plane crashed yesterday on top of a school. Thankfully, there were no children inside then. There was a small fire, and a few people were killed. The Germans sprayed the airmen with bullets as they parachuted down. The Amsterdammers who witnessed this ghastly act boiled with rage. We were scared out of our wits. How I hate the sound of gunfire!

Mr. Bolkestein, the Cabinet Minister, spoke on the Dutch broadcast from London. He stated that a collection of diaries and letters would be made after the war. Everyone jumped on my diary. But think how interesting it would be if I published a novel about the Secret Annex someday. The very title would make people assume that it was a detective story.

On a serious note, ten years after the war, people would really find it funny to read how we lived and spoke about as Jews in hiding. No matter how much I tell you, you'd still know very little about our lives. Last Sunday, the women were so scared during the air raid when 350 British planes dropped 550 tons of bombs. The houses shook under the onslaught like blades of grass in a hurricane. You know nothing about the epidemics here, and it would take me the entire day to describe these matters in full detail. People stand in a queue to buy vegetables and goods. Doctors are unable to visit patients as their vehicles are stolen as soon as their backs are turned. Thefts and burglaries are so common that you ask yourself why the Dutch have suddenly become so light-fingered. Eight and eleven-year-olds smash the windows of homes and steal whatever they can grab. People are scared to leave their homes unattended even for five minutes, and the newspapers are full of reward notices for stolen goods. Even the electronic clocks on the street corners haven't been spared, and the public phones have been stripped to the last wire.

The Dutch morale isn't good overall as everyone's hungry, and a week's ration doesn't last two days except for ersatz coffee. The invasion has been delayed, and men are being shipped to Germany. The children are ill and undernourished, and everyone's wearing worn-out clothes and run-down shoes. Few shoemakers are willing to repair shoes, and even if they do, one must wait for four months for the shoes to be repaired. There is also the risk of them disappearing.

The good news is that all this has led to the rise of acts of sabotage against the authorities.

THE DUTCH NEWS
GERMAN TROOPS OCCUPY HUNGARY

Thankfully, only a small percentage of the Dutch population is on the wrong side.

Yours, Anne

MARCH 31, 1944

Dear Kitty,

It's cold and yet most people have been without coal for a month. How awful that sounds, doesn't it? But there's great optimism about the Russian front, because that offers good news. The Russians have reached the Polish border and the Prut River in Romania. Close to Odessa, they've encircled Ternopol. We're expecting an extra communique from Stalin every night.

The Germans have occupied Hungary however, and that spells doom for the million Jews residing there. Nothing special is happening here. It's Mr. van Daan's birthday today, and he's received two packets of tobacco, a serving of coffee, lemon punch, sardines, eau de cologne, lilacs, tulips and a cake with raspberry

filling. It's a bit gluey because of the absence of butter and the poor quality of flour. But it's still delicious.

It's unlike me, but I'm going to describe the food situation in detail as it's a matter of both importance and difficulty not only at the Annex, but also throughout Holland, Europe and beyond. We've been through numerous 'food cycles' in our twenty-one month stay here. A 'food cycle' is a period which involves only one type of dish or vegetable to eat. We had only endive and nothing else for a long time. This was followed by spinach, kohlrabi, salsify, cucumbers, tomatoes, sauerkraut, etc., etc.

It's not great fun when you must eat something like sauerkraut every day for lunch and dinner. But when one is hungry, one does a lot of things. But now we're experiencing the most wonderful period so far, as there are no vegetables at all.

Our weekly lunch menu is made up of brown beans, split-pea soup, potatoes with

dumplings, potato kugel, and thanks to God, turnip greens or rotten carrots. Then, it's back to brown beans. Because of the bread shortage, we have potatoes for every meal. But we fry them a bit. There are brown beans in everything, including soup and bread. There are potatoes for dinner with imitation gravy and beet salad that we still have thankfully. We make dumplings with government-issue flour, yeast and water. They are gluey and hard and feel like rocks in your stomach.

The high point is the weekly slice of liverwurst, and the taste of jam on unbuttered bread. We are still alive, and mostly it still tastes good as well.

Yours, Anne

MONOPOLY
GO

Chapter Twelve

Break-in

APRIL 11, 1944

My dearest Kitty,

My head's swimming, and I really don't know where to begin. Everything was normal when I last wrote to you on Thursday. We played Monopoly on Friday and Saturday afternoon. The days passed by rather quickly. On Saturday, around 2 p.m., heavy machine-gun firing began. Everything was quiet otherwise.

The warehouse was broken into at nine-thirty. Father, Mr. van Daan and Peter were downstairs instantly as we women

waited. Four frightened women need to talk, and that's what we did till we heard a bang downstairs. Everything was quiet after that, and we remained calm even though we were scared out of our wits. What was that bang? Where were the men?

We heard footsteps on the stairs at ten o'clock. A pale and nervous Father entered, followed by Mr. van Daan.

"Lights out! Tiptoe upstairs. We're expecting the police!" he whispered. This wasn't a moment to display fear, and we went upstairs. No one told us what had happened as the men returned downstairs, returning only at ten past ten. Two of them kept watch at Peter's open window as the door to the landing was locked with the book-case shut. We covered our night-light with a sweater, and then they told us what had happened.

Peter had heard two loud bangs when he was on the landing. Going downstairs, he saw a large panel missing from the left part of the warehouse door. Rushing upstairs, he alerted the 'Home Guard', and the four of them went downstairs. They entered the warehouse to see the burglars busy in their act.

"Police!" Mr. van Daan screamed without thinking, and the burglars fled. The board was replaced in the door, so the gap wouldn't be noticeable to the police. But a swift kick from outside sent it flying back to the floor. The men were stunned at the burglars' audacity. Mr. van Daan angrily slammed an axe against the floor, and everything was silent after that. The panel was replaced again, and the burglary attempt foiled.

Suddenly, a man and a woman shone a flashlight through the opening, illuminating the entire warehouse. All four men raced upstairs, behind the bookcase. Undoubtedly, the man and the woman outside had alerted the police. It was Easter Sunday, and that meant that the next day, Easter Monday, was a holiday and the office would be closed.

That meant that we had to be perfectly still till Tuesday morning now. Think of the pain of having to sit in a terrified state in pitch darkness for a day and two nights! Mrs. van D had switched off the lamp in her fear.

It was eleven, and there was no sound. Father and Mr. van Daan took turns coming upstairs to us. We heard a noise below at eleven fifteen. We didn't move an inch and the only noise we heard was our own breathing. We heard footsteps in the house, the private office, the kitchen, and finally on the staircase. There were no sounds of breathing now, and only our hearts pounded! There was a rattling on the bookcase, and I cannot describe that moment. "We're done for now!" I whispered, as visions of the Gestapo dragging us away haunted me. The bookcase was rattled again twice, and a can fell. Then, the footsteps receded. We were safe, as of now. Everyone shivered, and I heard many sets of teeth chattering, although no one uttered a word.

We remained like this till eleven-thirty and heard no more sounds within the house. But a light shone at our landing, bang in front of the bookcase. There was no one in the building, but maybe someone stood guard outside. We tried to guess what was happening although we were scared. Then, we used the bathroom in turns. All the buckets were in the attic, and all we had was Peter's metal wastepaper basket. It was midnight, and we were all fatigued.

We lay down on the floor to sleep, and I was so tired I dozed off at two-thirty, only to wake up an hour later.

"We should hide the radio," Mrs. van D moaned.

"In the stove," Mr. van D suggested. "But if they find us they'll find it as well."

"They'll also find Anne's diary," Father added.

"Burn it," the most scared member of the group suggested.

This was the scariest moment along with the rattling on the bookcase. Not my diary! If that goes, so do I! Thank God Father didn't

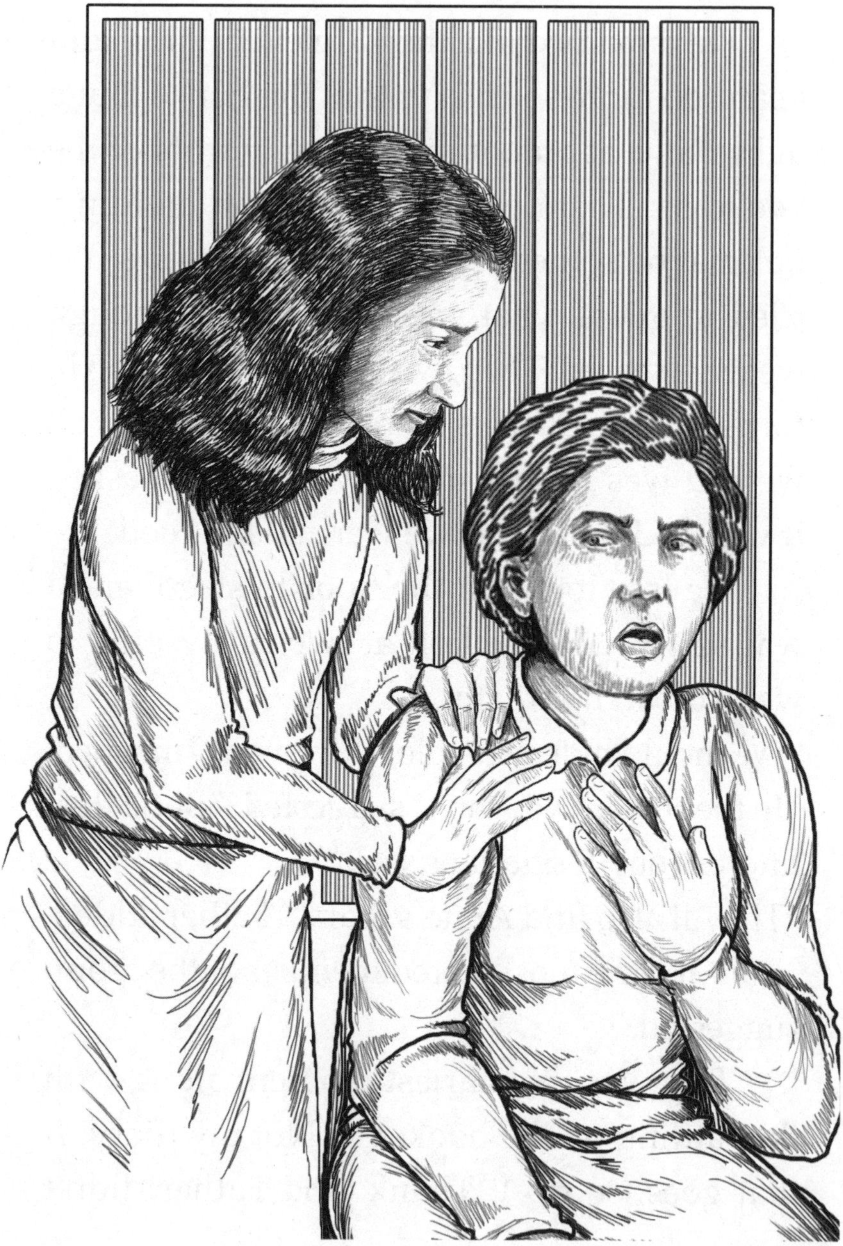

say anything after that. I comforted Mrs. van Daan, who was scared to death. We spoke about escape, Gestapo interrogation, calling Mr. Kleiman, and being brave, among other things. "We must act like soldiers, Mrs. van Daan. If our time has arrived, so be it. It'll be for Queen and Country, for freedom, truth and justice, as they are always telling us on the radio," I preached.

Soon it was five-thirty. I sat with Peter by his window and listened. We sat so close to each other that we felt each other's body trembling. I'm attaching the list that the men had made for Mr. Kleiman.

Burglary: Police in building, up to bookcase, but no farther. Burglars interrupted, forced warehouse door and fled through garden. Main entrance bolted; Kugler may have left through second door.

Typewriter and adding machine safe in black chest in private office.

Laundry in washtub in the kitchen.

Only Bep or Kugler have key to second door; lock may be broken.

Warn Jan and get key, inspect office; also feed cat.

Everything else went according to plan as Mr. Kleiman was phoned. Then we waited for either Jan or the police. Suddenly, we heard loud footsteps below, and everyone thought it was the police. "It's Jan," I said confidently. There was a knocking at our bookcase, and we held our breaths. Mrs. van Daan sank on her chair, almost fainting with the sheer tension.

Jan and Miep arrived to be greeted with shouts and tears. Nailing a pine wood board over the gap in the door, Jan left with Miep to report the break-in to the police. Miep had also discovered a note slipped under the door by the night watchman, Sleegers, who had also alerted the police. Jan intended to meet Sleegers.

We just had half an hour to put the house and ourselves in order. It was a magical transformation in just thirty minutes. Jan returned at eleven, and had the following story: Sleegers was asleep, but his wife informed Jan how her husband had discovered the hole while on his rounds. Fetching a policeman, the two had searched the building. As night watchman, Sleegers patrols the area every night on his bike, accompanied by two dogs. He would come and tell Mr. Kugler the rest on Tuesday, as per his wife. No one in the police station knew anything about the break-in, but they would come on Tuesday morning to investigate.

Jan met Mr. van Hoeven, our potato supplier, and informed him about the break-in. "I know," Hoeven replied calmly. "Last night, my wife and I noticed the gap in the door when we walked past your building. I peeked in with a flashlight, and that's when the burglars must have fled. I didn't call the police to be on the safer side as it wouldn't have been sensible in your case."

Mr. van Hoeven obviously guesses we are here, as he always delivers the potatoes at lunchtime. A good man!

By the time Jan left, and we did the dishes, it was one o'clock. All eight of us went to bed. I woke up at quarter to three and met Peter downstairs. We decided to meet in the office a little later after freshening up.

"You still dare to go to the front attic after all that's happened?" Peter asked me. I nodded, took my pillow, and we went up together. The weather was lovely, and even with the air-raid sirens blaring after a while, we stayed there. We put our arms around each other's shoulders, staying there till four, when Margot arrived to fetch us for coffee. That evening I thanked Peter for being the bravest of us all. We overcame that danger that night truly because God was watching over us. That incident brought about a lot of changes. Dussel will be carrying on with his work in the bathroom now, and Peter's patrolling duties in the house will be from eight-thirty to nine-thirty at night. Peter cannot keep his window open anymore as one of the Keg people had noticed that it was open. Neither

can we flush the toilet after nine-thirty at night. Sleegers has been hired as night watchman, and a carpenter from the underground is arriving tonight to create a barricade out of our white Frankfurt bedsteads.

Mr. Kugler has scolded us for our carelessness, and Jan has forbidden us from going downstairs. We must decide if Sleegers can be trusted, if the dogs will bark hearing someone behind the door, and how to create barricades. This incident has served as a strong reminder to us that we are Jews in chains, chained to a spot, without any human rights but with numerous obligations. Setting aside our emotions and feelings, we've to be brave and resolute, bear discomfort without complaining, and have faith in God. One day, these war clouds shall blow over. The time shall arrive when we will be treated as people again instead of just Jews.

Who has brought this pain upon us? Who has segregated us from the rest? It is God who has made us the way we are, and it is God who

shall save us. Maybe our religion will one day teach the world about goodness, and perhaps that's the reason why we suffer now for a larger cause. We can never be just Dutch or just English, but we shall always be Jews as well. But we shall continue being brave and strong. Only the weak fail while the strong survive!

But that night I thought I was going to die. I was ready to give my life for my country. But now that I have been spared, my first wish after this war is over is to be a Dutch citizen. I love this country and its people, and if I must, I shall write to the Queen herself to achieve this goal. I'm becoming more and more independent of my parents. I'm sure what I want now as I have a goal. I also have opinions, love, and a religion. I know I am a woman; a woman with inner strength and courage. If God lets me survive, I'll achieve much more than my mother. I shall step into this world and work for mankind, as all you need is courage and happiness.

Yours, Anne

Chapter Thirteen

The Rise of Anti-Semitism

APRIL 15, 1944

Dear Kitty,

We're all tense as it seems we've run out of luck. The toilet's leaking, and the faucet's stuck. But we should get these repaired soon thanks to our numerous connections. But one bad thing after the other keeps on happening. Peter forgot to unbolt the front door. So, Mr. Kugler and the warehouse employees couldn't get in. He went to Keg's, smashed in our office kitchen window, and entered. The Keg people saw the open windows in the

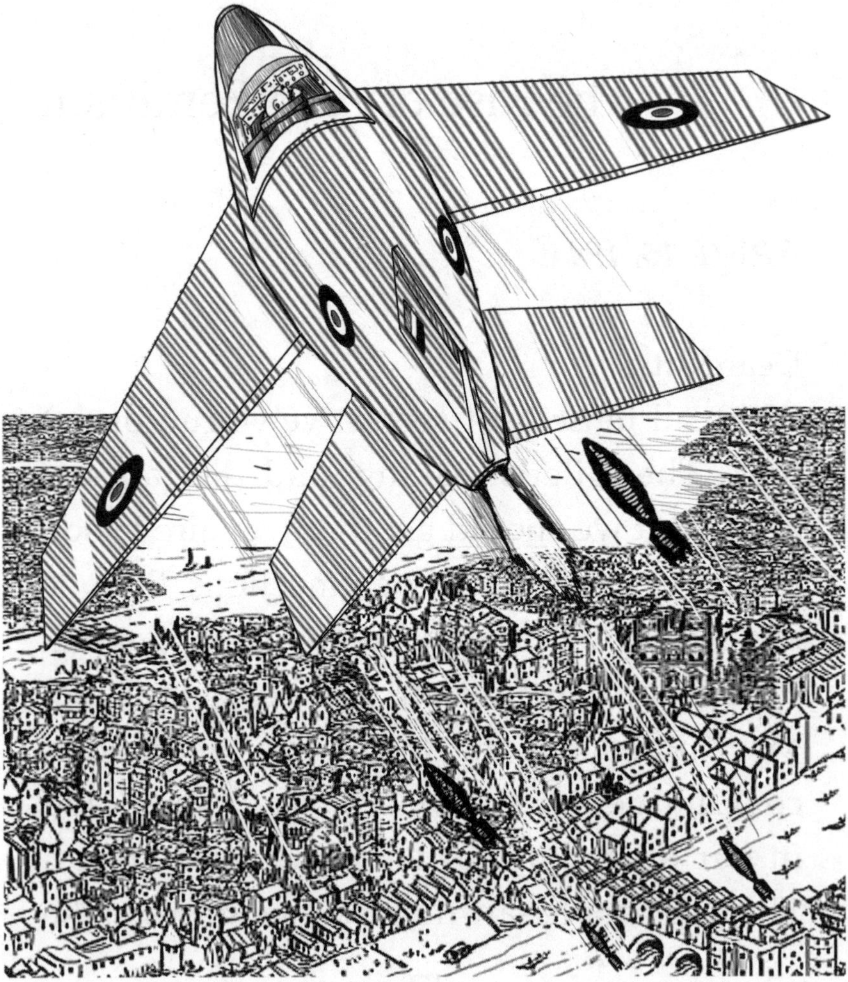

Annex as well. What could they be thinking? van Maaren too?

Mr. Kugler's very angry. We accuse him of not doing a thing to reinforce the doors, and then we do a silly thing like this! Peter's very upset, and almost began to cry. I think we are to be blamed equally as every day we check with him if he's unbolted the door which we didn't do. I think I'll go and comfort Peter later. The good news is that Mr. Kleiman is feeling much better and will see a specialist soon. Hopefully, he won't need an operation.

The Russians have occupied more than half the Crimea. The British aren't advancing beyond Cassino. Many heavy air raids have happened. The Registry of Births, Deaths and Marriages in the Hague was bombed. New ration registration cards will be issued to all Dutch people. Dussel and Mr. van Daan haven't been on talking terms for ten days now because of the new security measures after the break-in. One of them was that he's not allowed to go downstairs in the evening anymore. Peter and Mr. van Daan make the last round at nine-thirty every night. After that, no one can go downstairs. No one is allowed to flush the toilet after eight in the night or after eight in the morning. The windows can only be opened in the morning after the lights are on in Mr. Kugler's office. They cannot be prodded open with a stick at night, and this is the main reason why Dussel is sulking. He blames Mr. van Daan for this, saying he can live without food, but not without fresh air. He insists on finding a way to keep the windows open. Dussel is also not allowed to sit in Mr. Kugler's office on Saturday afternoons and Sundays anymore because the manager at Keg's might hear him if he's next door. Dussel defied this rule and sat there, making Mr. van Daan furious.

Father had a word with Dussel, who gave a funny excuse. Now, Father's keeping his interactions with Dussel limited as he insulted

Father. To think that it's the miserable man's birthday next week! How can you celebrate your birthday when you're sulking all the time? How can you accept gifts from people when you aren't even speaking to them? Mr. Voskuijl's condition is deteriorating rapidly. He's had a temperature of almost a hundred and a four for more than ten days now. The doctor says that it's a hopeless condition as the cancer has spread to his lungs. We'd like to help the poor man, but only God can save him now.

I've written a funny story titled 'Blurry the Explorer', which was a big hit with my listeners. I have a bad cold which I've passed on to Margot, Mother and Father.

Yours, Anne

MAY 3, 1944

Dear Kitty,

For the past two weeks, we are having lunch at eleven-thirty on Saturdays. The only thing

we have in the mornings is a cup of hot cereal as that saves a meal. It's still difficult to get vegetables, and we had rotten boiled lettuce this afternoon. Ordinary lettuce, spinach and boiled lettuce are all there is. Add rotten potatoes to that, and you have a meal fit for a king! "What's the point of war? Why can't people live together in peace? Why is there so much destruction"? The question is a fair one, but so far no one has provided a satisfactory answer. Why is England making bigger planes and bombs and at the same time making new houses for reconstruction? Why are countries spending millions on the war instead of spending it on medical science, artists or the poor? Why are people in one part of the world starving when heaps of food are rotting away in another part of the world? Why are people so crazy? I think the war is the brainchild of politicians and capitalists. Oh yes, the common man is as guilty, for not having rebelled long ago.

There's a destructive urge in people, the urge to kill! Until the whole of humanity witnesses a metamorphosis, wars will be waged continuously, and everything that has been carefully cultivated and developed will be destroyed. Then, we will have to start from zero! But we can hardly believe the prices of things in the outside world now. Half a pound of tea costs 350.00 guilders, 80 guilders for the same amount of coffee, a pound of butter 35.00 guilders, an egg 1.45 guilders. An ounce of Bulgarian tobacco costs as much as 14.00 guilders. Black market trading is engaged in by everyone. Break-ins, murders and thefts are common, and even the police and the night watchmen are getting in on the act. Salaries have been frozen and as no one wants to stay hungry, they are resorting to crime. The police are having a tough task trying to track down teenaged girls reported missing every day.

Yours, Anne

MAY 9, 1944

Dear Kitty,

Mr. Kugler told us today that Mrs. Broks wanted to spend two hours in the office every afternoon from Monday. Imagine that! The office staff won't be able to come upstairs, and the potatoes won't be delivered. We won't be able to move around or go to the bathroom.

My biggest wish is to be a journalist, and a famous writer after that. After the war, I want to publish a book called the Secret Annex. I don't know if I'll succeed, but my diary can be the basis. Yesterday was Father's birthday, Father and Mother's nineteenth wedding anniversary, and a day without the cleaning lady. The sun was shining like it never did before in 1944. Our chestnut tree is in full bloom, beautifully covered in leaves.

Everyone is talking about the invasion. The whole of Europe is talking about it, but sadly, the invasion hasn't even begun. Our beloved

Queen addressed the country on Tuesday and Wednesday evening. She's on vacation currently so she'll be in good health when she eventually returns to the Netherlands. She used words like 'soon, when I'm back in Holland', 'a swift liberation', 'heroism', and 'heavy burdens'. Prime Minister Gerbrandy's speech followed. He has such a squeaky little child's voice. A clergyman concluded by asking God to take care of the Jews in concentration camps, prisons or working in Germany. The suspense has reached fever pitch now. The good Dutch people haven't kept their faith in the English as not everyone thinks that the English bluff is a brilliant strategical move. No one thought about the fact that the British are fighting for their own interests. It's not their duty to save Holland, as everyone here assumes. Why should the English help us? The English are as much to be blamed for the war as the countries occupied by the Germans now. The British were sleeping when Germany was rearming themselves. But

then, so were all the other countries, especially the ones bordering on Germany. Now, all these countries, especially England, are paying a heavy price for having buried their heads in the sand for so long in a case of ostrich policy. No country will sacrifice its men without reason. England will choose the date of invasion and liberation, not the occupied territories.

We are greatly dismayed as anti-Semitism has risen in circles where it is unthinkable. The Christians feel that the Jews are divulging their secrets to the Germans. Even if this were true, would the Christians have acted differently had they been in our place? Underground circles are saying that German Jews who immigrated to Holland before the war and now have been sent to Poland, shouldn't be allowed to return here. They had been granted the right to asylum in Holland, but once Hitler is gone, they should return to Germany. After hearing that, one wonders why we are fighting this war. For freedom, truth and justice? Well, the war isn't

JEWS GO BACK
JODEN GAAN TERUG
NO JEWS IN HOLLAND
GEEN JODEN IN HOLAND

over yet, and Jews are considered as lesser human beings. That adage has been confirmed yet again: "What one Christian does is his own responsibility, what one Jew does, reflects on all Jews".

It's not understandable how the Dutch, a nation of good, honest, upright people can pass judgment on us, the most oppressed, hapless and pitiable people in the world. I hope that this anti-Semitism is a passing phase. But if the Dutch do carry out this threat, the handful of Jews left in Holland will have to abandon this beautiful country, which once gave us shelter, and now turns its back on us. I love Holland! I hoped once that it would be a fatherland to me, as I lost my own. I still hope so.

Yours, Anne

Chapter Fourteen

D-Day

MAY 25, 1944

Dear Kitty,

Mr. van Hoeven was arrested today morning for hiding two Jews in his house. It's a big blow for us, because those poor Jews are doomed, and so is Mr. van Hoeven. The world's turned upside down, as good people are being sent to concentration camps and prisons. The lowest of the low are ruling and unless you are a Nazi, your fate is uncertain. Losing Mr. van Hoeven is a big loss because Bep can't carry such huge amounts of potatoes here, and we eat less now.

Mother says we will skip breakfast, have hot cereal and bread for lunch and fried potatoes for dinner. We shall have vegetables or lettuce once or twice a week. Staying hungry is better than being caught.

Miep and Mr. Kugler share the burden for our responsibility, and the latter can barely speak from the tension and the strain. Mr. Kleiman and Bep have their own worries, the former with his health and the latter with her engagement. Their tension is relieved somewhat by meeting their friends. But we've never experienced relief in these two years here. One afternoon, Miep came up and asked Father if we thought that they were also anti-Semitic like the rest. A stunned Father talked her out, but they are going out of the way for us now. They are such good, noble people. Oh, let something happen soon! Even an air raid! Nothing can be as bad as this worry. Let the end come, no matter how cruel it is.

Yours, Anne

JUNE 6, 1944

Dear Kitty,

"It's D-DAY!" the BBC announced at twelve. The invasion has begun. The British reported heavy bombing of Calais, Boulogne, LeHavre, Cherbourg, and Pas de Calais at eight this morning. As a precautionary measure for those residing within twenty miles from the coast in the occupied areas, there was a warning to be alert for bombardments. The British would drop pamphlets an hour earlier wherever possible.

German news has reported that British paratroopers have landed on the French coast. "British landing crafts are engaged in combat with German naval units," the BBC reports. In his speech to the French people on BBC, Supreme Commander General Dwight Eisenhower said, "Stiff fighting will come now, but after this, the victory. Good luck." According to the BBC, 11,000 planes, 4,000 landing crafts and small boats have been deployed in action by British and American forces.

There is total commotion in the Annex. Is this really the beginning of the much-awaited liberation? Will 1944 bring us victory and freedom? We don't have the answer, but where there's hope, there is life. It's salvation for not just us Jews, but for all of Holland and occupied Europe. Margot says we might return to school in September or October. Last night and today morning, straw and rubber dummies were air-dropped behind German lines, exploding as soon as they hit the ground. Paratroopers, with their faces blackened so they couldn't be seen in the dark, landed as well. 5,500 tons of bombs hit the French coast in the night, and the first landing craft arrived ashore at six in the morning. But the German coastal batteries were destroyed even before the landing.

Yours, Anne

JUNE 13, 1944

Dearest Kitty,

I'm fifteen now that another birthday has gone by. The invasion is going splendidly despite the terrible weather – rains, gale winds and high seas. Churchill, Smuts, Eisenhower and Arnold visited the liberated French villages yesterday. Churchill rode on a torpedo boat that shelled the coast. Unlike many men, he doesn't know the meaning of fear, an enviable trait.

It's not easy to judge the mood of the Dutch from our position at the Annex. There's no doubt that many are happy at the arrival of the British. But many say that they don't want to be occupied by the British. They are being very unfair as their sole reasoning is that England should fight and sacrifice her sons to liberate Holland. But after that, they should return to their own country. But what would have happened to Holland and its

neighbours if England had signed a peace treaty with Germany? Holland would have become German, and that would have been an end of all things. All the Dutch critics and haters of the British should be given a good shaking like one would plump up a pillow. That would put their jumbled brains in order!

Why does everyone think I'm arrogant? Am I arrogant, or are they? Mrs. van Daan and Dussel, two of my main accusers, are actually just plain stupid. Stupid people normally can't bear it when others do something better than they do. Mrs. van Daan thinks I'm stupid because I don't suffer from stupidity as much as she does. The same applies for Dussel. But as they say, 'There's no smoke without fire." I accept that I'm a know-it-all. But I'm more critical about myself than anyone else. The most popular Anne refrain is: "No one understands me!" If only there was someone who took my feelings seriously. Alas, I haven't found that person yet, and must keep searching. Am I

in love with nature because I haven't been outdoors for so long? Few are isolated from nature as we are, and the joys of nature can be shared by the rich and poor alike. Not only does nature spark my imagination, but staring at the stars, sky and the moon calms me down and makes me hopeful. Nature is the best medicine!

One question that has bothered me often is that why are women considered inferior to men? While it's easy to say it's unfair, I'd like to understand the reason for this grave injustice. Obviously, men dominated women because of their greater physical strength. Women went along with this silently until recent times, which was stupid, as a problem is rooted deeper the longer it continues. Thankfully, education, progress and work have been an eye-opener for women. They have been granted equal rights in many countries, and even men have realised that it was unfair to treat women this way. Modern women want the right to be completely independent.

But women should be respected as well. Why can't women be soldiers? During childbirth, a woman suffers more pain than a war hero. But what does she get in return for enduring that pain? Disfigured after giving birth, she's pushed aside, abandoned by her children, and eventually her beauty fades. Women are much tougher than all the war heroes and freedom-fighters put together. I'm not implying that women should stop having children, as that is nature's way. I'm condemning our system of values, and the men who don't acknowledge the greatness of women and their contribution to our society.

Yours, Anne

Chapter Fifteen

Peter Falls in Love

JUNE 23, 1944

Dear Kitty,

There's nothing special happening here. The British have begun an all-out attack on Cherbourg. Mr. van Daan is sure we'll be liberated before October 10. The Russians have joined the campaign, beginning their offensive near Vitebsk. The date is exactly three years to the date Germany invaded Russia. We have almost run out of potatoes and will count them out for each person from now on so that each can do what they want with them.

Cherbourg, Vitebsk and Zhlobin fell today, and the mood has changed. Five German generals were killed near Cherbourg, and two taken prisoner. The British have got a harbour now and can bring whatever they want on shore. Just five weeks after the invasion, the entire Cotentin Peninsula has been captured. What an achievement! Three weeks since D-Day not a single day has passed without rain and storms. But this hasn't stopped the British and Americans from proving their might. The Germans must be really shaking in their boots now because the Bolsheviks are getting closer.

All German women, except the ones employed in the military, are being evacuated along with their children from the coastal regions to the provinces. The leader of the Dutch National Socialist (Nazi) Party has announced that he'll enlist if the war reaches Holland. Is that fat pig planning to fight? Why didn't he do that in Russia before? The war is going wonderfully well and spirits are rising.

The van Daans are doing disappearing acts with the sugar, Bep's changed her hairstyle, and Miep's taken a week off.

Yours, Anne

JULY 6, 1944

Dearest Kitty,

Peter's beginning to lean on me, and I don't want that. How can I make him understand that while it might seem easy and nice, it will drag him down to a depth where he will never be able to rise again? Peter's problem is that he doesn't have a goal in life, and he thinks he's too stupid and inferior to achieve anything. He's never known what it feels like to make someone else happy, and I'm afraid I can't teach him that. Peter's not religious, and scoffs at Jesus Christ. I'm not Orthodox, but it hurts to see him in that lonely and wretched state. Religious people should be glad as they are blessed to believe in a higher order. Religion also keeps a person on the right path by following your own sense of honour and conscience rather than fearing the wrath of God.

A quiet conscience gives you strength.

Yours, Anne

What Do You
Think Of The
Modern Young Girl

Chapter Sixteen

Father and Mother don't Understand me

JULY 15, 1944

Dear Kitty,

We've received a book from the library titled, *What Do You Think of the Modern Young Girl?* I'd like to discuss this subject today. The writer criticises today's youth, accusing them of being obsessed with superficial things even though she believes that they will be the architects of a better, beautiful world. I felt sometimes that the writer was accusing me directly and would like to defend myself from this attack.

I have a lot of self-knowledge and can analyse my weaknesses just like I would do for a stranger. This self-awareness is so strong that I am often harsh on myself. Like Father says, 'Every child has to raise itself.' I also face life with a lot of bravery and can withstand the blows that life rains on me.

Now, I'd like to focus on the chapter, 'Father and Mother Don't Understand Me.' My parents have always spoiled me rotten, treated me kindly, and done what all parents can. Despite that I've felt lonely and neglected. Father tried in vain to change my rebellious spirit. But why didn't he help me in my struggle? The truth is that he used the wrong methods. He always spoke to me like a child going through a difficult phase in life. He overlooked the fact that this struggle to emerge triumphant over my difficulties was the most important thing in my life. I didn't want to be treated like other girls, but as Anne-in-her-own-right, and he never understood that. Hence, I've purposely

alienated myself from him. It was egotistical, but I had to do that to be at peace with myself and avoid being irritable with him.

But a bigger disappointment is Peter. I think a lot about Peter as he was my conquest, and not the other way around. I visualised him as a sweet, innocent boy in need of love and companionship. I needed someone to pour out my heart to and needed a friend badly. But the intimacy that developed seems outrageous to me now. We spoke about intimate things, but never about those closest to my heart. The fatal mistake I made was using intimacy to get closer to him, thus ruling out other forms of friendship. Now, he likes me with each passing day.

I think the problems in the Annex has more impact on us younger people than the older ones. We are too young to handle these problems, and yet they are thrust upon us. But I still cling on to my ideals even though they seem impractical and absurd now. That's because I

firmly believe that people are still good at heart. I can feel that this chaos will destroy us too one day but am hopeful that this cruelty will end one day, with the return of peace. Maybe on that day my ideals will be realised!

Yours, Anne

The Minneapolis Morning Tribune
HITLER SURVIVES IN AN ASSASSINATION ATTEMPT
DUITSCHLAND
HITLER OVERLEEFT MOORDAANSLAG

Chapter Seventeen

Hitler Survives

JULY 21, 1944

Great news! I'm optimistic now. An assassination attempt has been made on Hitler's life, and that too by a German general. Divine Providence saved the Fuhrer's life, who received minor burns and scratches. The head of the conspiracy has been shot, but Hitler's own men are fed up of this war and would like to see the end of Hitler. It also means less work for the British and the Americans if the Germans kill each other.

Hitler has now put all military personnel under the Gestapo, with orders that if any

soldier learns of his superior's involvement on Hitler's life, he may shoot his superior on sight. What a fine kettle of fish that will be! Little Johnny's feet are sore after a long March and his commanding officer punishes him. "You tried to kill the Fuhrer," Little Johnny shouts angrily, grabbing his rifle and shooting his snooty officer. "Take that!"

All officers fear their soldiers, as soldiers are apparently more powerful than their officers now.

Yours, Anne

A BUNDLE OF CONTRADICTIONS

Chapter Eighteen

Contradiction

AUGUST 1, 1944

Dear Kitty,
They call me, 'A bundle of contradictions'. What does 'contradiction' mean? It can be interpreted in two ways like so many words: a contradiction imposed from within and imposed from without. The latter means always knowing the best, not accepting the opinions of others, and having the last word. Those are the negative traits I've been classified under. The former, which is known to others, is my secret. I'm split into two as mentioned before. One side is my extrovert self,

and just because no one knows Anne's other and better side, most people can't stand me. I am just what a romantic movie is to a great thinker- a diversion, a comic interlude, something quickly forgotten. It's not bad, but not good either. My lighter, false side will always have an edge over my deeper side, and will always win. I've often tried to push away this flippant Anne, but it hasn't worked. This is because when I'm quiet and serious, people think that it is an act, and I've to save myself with another joke. I'm afraid of being mocked and not taken seriously when people who know me will discover my finer and better side. If only I could be what I want to be, and what I was capable of being. If only there were no other people in this world.

Yours, Anne

Chapter Nineteen

Afterword

A car pulled up between ten and ten-thirty at 263 Prinsengracht on the morning of August 4, 1944. Many figures stepped out, including an SS sergeant, Karl Josef Silberbauer and three armed Dutch members of the Security Police, in civilian clothes. Receiving a tip off, they arrested the eight people hiding in the Annex, and two of their helpers. They also took away all the valuables they could find.

Kugler and Kleiman were taken to a prison in Amsterdam and transferred without the benefit of a trial to a camp in Amersfoort (Holland) on September 11, 1944. Kleiman

was released on September 18 because of his ill-health and stayed in Amsterdam until his death in 1959. Kugler escaped from the prison on March 28, 1945, emigrating to Canada in 1955. He breathed his last in Toronto in 1989. Bep died in Amsterdam in 1983, and Miep died in Hoorn on January 11, 2010 at the age of 100. Her husband Jan passed away in 1993.

After their arrest, the eight members of the Annex were initially brought to a prison in Amsterdam, and then transferred to Westerbrok, the transit camp for Jews in North Holland. They were deported to Auschwitz (Poland) on September 3, 1944. According to Otto Frank's testimony, van Daan was gassed to death in October or November 1944, just before the gas chambers were dismantled. Mrs. van Daan was transported to many concentration camps from Auschwitz. It's certain she did not survive.

Peter van Daan was forced to participate in the 'death march' from Auschwitz to Mauthausen (Austria) on January 16, 1945, three days before

the camp was liberated. Albert Dussel and Edith Frank died as well. Margot and Anne Frank were transported from Auschwitz to Bergen Belsen, a concentration camp near Hannover (Germany).

Because of the horrible hygienic conditions, a typhus epidemic broke out in the winter of 1944-1945, killing thousand of prisoners. Anne died a few days after Margot, probably in late February or early March. Their bodies were possibly dumped in Bergen-Belsen's mass graves. British troops liberated the camp on April 12, 1945. Otto Frank was the only one among the eight to survive the concentration camps. He returned to Amsterdam on June 3, 1945 after Auschwitz was liberated by Russian troops. In 1953, he moved to Basel (Switzerland). He married Elfriede Markovits Geiringer, originally from Vienna, a survivor of Auschwitz, who had lost a son and a husband in Mauthausen.

Otto Frank devoted the rest of his life to sharing the message of his daughter's diary with people across the world until his death on August 19, 1980.

About the Author

■ Anne Frank (1929 - 1945)

Annelies Marie 'Anne' Frank (12 June 1929- Early March 1945) is the most talked about holocaust Jewish victims. Her wartime diary titled, *The Diary of a Young Girl* has inspired numerous films and plays. After her diary was published she got international fame, albeit posthumously. This diary documents her experiences in hiding when the Germans occupied Holland during World War II.

In 1933, the Frank family relocated to the Netherlands from Germany, and this was the very year when the Nazi Party wrested control over Germany. May 1940, the German occupation of the Netherlands saw the Franks trapped in Amsterdam. As the Jews were persecuted with enormous regularity from 1942, the Franks went into hiding for two years. They were betrayed and deported to concentration camps.

Otto Frank was the sole survivor, and he published his daughter's diary in 1947. Since then, it has been translated into many languages from the original Dutch. The diary chronicles Anne's life from 12 June 1942 until 1 August 1944.

■ List of Main Characters

Anne Frank: The writer of the diary, Anne is a young Dutch girl of German-Jewish origin and the youngest child of Mr. and Mrs. Frank. As the diary progresses, Anne is transformed from a spoiled, naive thirteen-year-old to a self-aware young woman. She spends two years in hiding with her family after the German occupation till being deported to a concentration camp, where she dies before her sixteenth birthday.

Margot Frank: Margot is Anne Frank's older sister. She is considered the supposed role model for Anne by her family and it is because of her call-up by the Gestapo that the Franks go into hiding. Margot dies a few weeks before Anne in the concentration camp.

Mrs. Frank: She's the mother of Anne and Margot Frank, and hails from a wealthy family. She fails Anne as a mother although she has a loving relationship with Margot.

Mr. Otto Frank: Mr. Frank is closest to his daughter Anne. The sole survivor from his family after the war, it is because of his efforts that Anne's diary was finally published.

Mr. van Daan: He is Mr. Frank's friend and business associate of Mr. Frank, who joins the Franks in hiding along with his family. He is eventually gassed at Auschwitz.

Mrs. van Daan: She is Mr. van Daan's wife, a vain woman who lacks humility.

Peter van Daan: Peter is the only son of Mr. and Mrs. van Daan. He is sixteen, shy, and awkward. Anne and Peter fall in love with each other, till Anne decides that he is weak and lacks character.

■ Questions

Chapter 1

- *What presents did Anne receive on her birthday? Which was her favourite present and why?*
- *Why does Anne write, "Paper has more patience than people"? Explain in detail.*

Chapter 2

- *Why did Anne's father decide to go into hiding with his family? Do you think this was a sensible decision? Explain.*
- *Describe the building where the Franks moved.*

Chapter 3

- *Why was Anne so keen to listen to the radio?*
- *What were the rumours that were floating around regarding the disappearance of the Franks?*

Chapter 4

- *Describe the bathing places of the different members of the Annex.*
- *Was Anne a German or was she Dutch? Give reasons for your answer.*

Chapter 5

- *Who was Churchill? How was his opinion different from that of the Dutch people?*
- *Who was the eighth person to arrive into hiding? How and why was he chosen?*

Chapter 6

- *Who was Dussel's first victim? Describe what happened during the dental appointment.*
- *What did Anne think of her housemates in the Annex?*

Chapter 7

- *What was the unfortunate news about Mr. Kleiman? Why was this news bad?*
- *Who was Mr. van Maaren? Why was he a threat to the members of the Annex?*

Chapter 8

- *Why did the van Daans wish to sell their belongings? Did they succeed? Why?*
- *Who was Hanneli? Why do you think Anne dreamt about Hanneli? Explain in detail.*

Chapter 9

- *What was Anne suffering from? What were the remedies applied?*
- *Why was Anne so angry with her mother? Explain in detail.*

Chapter 10

- *What was the name of the book everyone in the Annex was reading? Why did Mrs. Frank think it was a good book?*
- *What did the people in the Annex eat? Why did they have to eat such wretched food?*

Chapter 11

- *Where did the plane crash take place? Were there any casualties?*
- *Why was the morale of the Dutch people low?*

Chapter 12

- *Who broke into the Annex and why?*
- *Who was Mr. van Hoeven? Describe his conversation with Jan.*

Chapter 13

- *What was the mistake that Peter made? Do you think it was Peter's fault?*
- *What was Anne's opinion about the war?*

Chapter 14

- *Who arrested Mr. van Hoeven? Why was it a loss for the people in the Annex?*
- *Why did Anne think that the role of a soldier would suit women?*

Chapter 15

- *What was Peter's problem according to Anne?*
- *Why did Anne think that 'Nature' is the best medicine?*

Chapter 16

- *Why did Anne think that her parents didn't understand her?*
- *Why did the problems in the Annexe have more impact on younger people than the older ones?*

Chapter 17

- *Who tried to kill Hitler and why? Did he succeed?*
- *What are the two sides of a human being?*

Chapter 18

- *Explain in Anne's words the meaning of 'contradiction'.*
- *Why couldn't Anne be quiet and serious?*

Chapter 19

- *What misfortune fell upon the members of the Annex?*
- *What was the fate of the different members in the end?*